CLOUD-CUCKOO-LAND

by
Emmanuel Nwachukwu

All characters and events portrayed in this story are fictitious. Any similarity to persons living or dead is purely coincidental.

ISBN-10: 1545314209
ISBN-13: 978-1545314203

I WORSHIP THE SUPREMACY OF GOD

To My Valued Friend,
Precious(Vincent)Uwalaka

"Things your book just saw could be the plot for a sci-fi thriller.

After you uploaded your manuscript it bounced securely across web servers on into the cloud and docked safely on the U.S.S. Book Genome Project. Your Uniquely Original words, phrases, paragraphs and chapters were spliced and sent through time and space into the depths of the Genome; organized into logical themes and compared to the text of literary giants like Toni Morrison, Ernest Hemingway and Gabriel Marquez.

The profile you will find here is an elegant vision of marrying your art to Lulu's science.

Just like people, every book has its own unique personality. We hope you enjoy meeting yours for the first time"

—*WaNoWrimo*

I actually made certain this captivating book of mine did not miss my exceptional eclecticism in writing. **Cloud-Cuckoo-Land** *is of literary prowess and rightly removes the cost of hindsight—The painful understanding of an irreversible situation only after it has happened, and that means you would have done things different.*

...Emmanuel Nwachukwu.

Preamble...

*H*istory had shown that there were two kinds of angels; the good and the bad. The war that broke out in heaven was going to bring out the comparing dichotomy. Lucifer was the general that led the rebellious faction—thus the bad angels, while Michael was the general that led the loyal faction that kicked their strike force out of heaven—thus the good angels. History was impeccable, especially on its relationship with the first coup d'état that was accurately recorded in the holy bible. But here in the world of Eve, smart minds had discovered that history had actually missed an account of a certain angel. Another type of angel totally in a different league. While history omitted this particular account was still unknown. Maybe it was because of the non-alignment policy of this angel; or because of the controversial gender of this angel; or because of the paradoxical nature of this angel's mission. Whatever, history nearly killed the predestination of the chief inhabitant of this world, with that negligence in recognising the angel of contradictory nature.

In a corner this angel in a different league was considering missions poles apart from Michael's, Gabriel's, Cherubim's and seraphim's, Mr. Wyi Worri's quagmire on earth was captured.

From the vantage point of present, all the missions of this angel, from the time immemorial, achieved little; so the next task was going to be a huge landmark. Now this angel of controversial gender watched the target of mission again; he needed to be helped seriously. He was a nice guy of big dreams, only that these dreams were very close to delusions of grandeur—judging with things without. He was a paradox too, and that was what made him and the angel in a different league. Approve him or object him, bless him or cause him, he foolishly believed in his farfetched dreams for sole survival. In short, take him or leave him, that was his faith, and unbendingly he communicated it to everyone he met, which was one of the reasons why this angel in his league had picked him. The world thought he was a basket case; but he thought the world gave him witch-hunts. A certain amount of conformity was particularly required of an inhabitant of earth toeing her line of fate; but he was a dissenter. Mr. Wyi Worri was a malcontent.

He had a vision to own an ideal home; he had a vision to add peerless value to the literary world; but he lacked cooperate vision to see the countervailing vicissitude tantamount to end of the road. Just two years plus ago, he was standing long on the road, waiting to get a bike for his journey back to school, when he saw this angel on the ground of earth, walking towards him. He needed urgently a girlfriend to turn a wife and protect himself properly, so he calculated things quickly. This beautiful fair skinned robust angel from heaven had everything to offer; and he measured them. She was his complementary left and right. He always knew he had many faults about his build, and this angel was a make-up physique for him. In short, she was overall, voluptuous—and he followed her, leaving out his journey.

Just exactly one year after that, they climbed the numerous steps of St. Mary's Catholic Church, Okigwe, and had a certain secret marriage on their own. A secret marriage that was actually a vow of engagement. There was no law to give binding reason that this angel was going to be a faithful partner—since it was done before a priest-less altar. However, he gave her a name that he thought God had actually put in his mouth the very day he meet her. Her name was MyAngel.

Now, another one year, Mr. Wyi Worri was waiting for a visiting angel in the night, when there was blustery wind, and her bus was late to come by. It was a matter of anxiety, but Prince Williams, the corps member serving the nation with Mr. Wyi Worri, was an understanding companion. He was also an ex-seminarian that just had his philosophy before the theology, and felt it was nice to continue his work of sublimation as a laity rather. Sometimes Mr. Wyi Worri thought rudely, maybe the wicked combustion of continence burnt off his bud of chastity too early enough, before he could be ordained.

It was Ikare—Onitsha road, and buses were coming down from Onitsha; but she wasn't a passenger in any of them. Moment after moment. Then this particular helpful one arrived at the terminal park. An eighteen passenger seater bus. On the third seat, the one before the rear seat, a fair complexioned dish in the middle, with aura of beauty, was perceptible in the gloomy bus. A face that wasn't hard to recognize. Then a voice that exclaimed breathlessly, *'Sweetheart'*.

"Welcome, MyAngel!" Mr. Wyi Worri jubilated, darting his eyes for Prince Williams.

She hopped down and hopped to him, her arms going around his waist. Excessive affection. She buried her face around his shoulder. Her mien spoke of heavenly love, and was just nice. Just nice.

Later in the night, when only two of them were in his room, there wasn't, and had never been, any hardness about her. There was just lovingness. And passion. A crazy kind of passion. A wonderful kind of passion.

"Please, make love to me," she beseeched.

It was a warning all over his instinct and inside his head.

But not that suspicious, and no need for caveat.

He touched her, she was ready. Beauty of love. He reached his hand for a pack of durex.

"Leave the condom, sweetheart," she said. "Skin is intimate... and still better."

Much later, about two months added, long deep in the night, and he was counting neurotically, while other members of this lodge were deep asleep…

MyAngel visited on ninth January—Friday, and that same night we made love all through the night. No sex on tenth, Saturday. No sex on eleventh, Sunday. Well, this Sunday night MyAngel encountered an ailment that tried to block her heartbeat, and Prince Williams had alerted the entire compound, and Mr. Clement, another close corps member, was so obliging to gather all the occupants of this lodge of corps members, and like a deadweight, they carried her to the hospital that early hours of day Monday.

No sex on twelfth, the Monday night, ipso facto. We made love on thirteenth, Tuesday, at Cynthia's place, another close lady corps member. No sex again till sixteenth, Friday evening—that day I supposed to attend a corps members' football competition. She went back to Lagos on the following day, Saturday.

From ninth till now is seventy one days. From thirteenth till now is sixty seven days, and from sixteenth till now is sixty four days…

Was Mr. Wyi Worri actually a basket-case?

Chapter One

" *W* hat?"

MyAngel said; (So you're going to deny your baby?) She was referring to his question. (Strewth! That's unsavoury, Mister Wyi Worri)

"No, lady, just that it's a bit little surprise; like unimaginable... like um... you tell me this when..."

(What unimaginable? That you squirted your semen inside me at the wrong time of the month?) She snapped. (Mister Wyi Worri, you need to keep your unguarded thoughts under control. *Jesus*, they're ingrate personified! You know!)

"Right, lady, right."

The line was angrily cut at the other end and Mr. Wyi Worri picked his books and beat a retreat, leaving his students sitting there wondering in perplexity.

Even after two months anxiety of his prospect of fathering a baby, he still let the unthinkable inkling follow and get to him. Allowing them touch that naked wire responsible for triggering doubting mechanism. Reaching the staffroom shared by the corps members serving the nation here in this school, he threw the books over the table with every ounce of bitter feeling he had gathered, picked his sunglass and left without exchanging or leaving any word with his colleagues. He walked into the sun going away. The same pointing instinct, the same pointing suspicion, the same impelling fact kept reappearing mechanically. The system was arousing them out like when a home-truth was irrepressible.

Seeing a phone booth under a parasol, and a redemptive-worth thought flashing inside him, he crossed towards it.

"Lady, what about removing it?" he suggested, seeing his present position.

(No!)the curt reply. (I can't abort the baby. I conceived it with genuine motive, and it's a product of love. Mister Wyi Worri, it's a blessing; it's love.)

The line was cut again from the other end, and Mr. Wyi Worri was thinking; *I conceive it with genuine motive*, by who? *It's love*, but of whom really? He was a confused case. He had compromised virtually all his footloose and fancy-free. For this lady, he had rearranged his life. What he wanted was rectitude in his engagement, where her love would only register with him without dent. Pure and blameless. He wanted dividends of love only on true unsullied bliss and sacred union. He wanted the cutesiest partner, a willing beautiful lover, but more than anything he wanted a trustworthy wife. At least he wanted some inamorata, who would give value to his costly painstaking celibacy to some vows. Some inamorata that was totally in for him.

But it seemed he had unfortunately plight his throat with an errant lover. So far sacredness of love was concerned, one who wanted nothing integrity. Maybe she didn't know love really, and then aspired to nothing, as she had now accomplished nothing with that controversial pregnancy. *Gawd*, should he say from another man? Maybe he didn't want his own MyAngel anymore—his vowed wife-to-be? Not as a blast bunch of betrayal! But this was something that started with genuine mesmerizing promises and luminescence of love. Words hadn't needed anymore. They had shown in their eyes and displayed in their emotions. It wasn't anything like mickey-mousy involvement. They had on their own taken those vows and sealed it with passionate kisses there at the altar. No priest was there, but they believed God was present as their witness.

And then they went home that evening and perfected the conjugal promises with that sacrosanct consummation of love. He meant, still with the numinousness. The high divine sense of presence of God. Call it *expensive engagement,* pooh, they wouldn't care. Call it *secret marriage,* oops-a-dairy, then they were waiting to present their parents with a fait accompli at the right time—but look at her now; he shook his head disgustedly.

He looked around with the awareness of weather. Glancing at the surface of his handset, he realized that it was almost the time to dismiss the school for the day—the need of going home from there. Now, to hell with his primary assignment of this NYSC programme! He wasn't in the mood. Damned, really he wasn't.

He crossed the road and thumbed a bus heading to Ayepe. En route his thoughts compete with two countervailing thoughts—a possible looming outcome, and a possible divine outcome. The crude inkling momentarily was replaced with the inspiring struggling contending thought. He separated it to a clean corner of his psyche and upheld it. To keep up with the Joneses, it was one of those wishful thoughts that played prevalent part in all his prayers all through his teens, the stripling and this period of adulthood. Last year November was his twenty seven. This year ushered him to twenty eight, and the next twenty nine and then thirty. The anticipated fulfilling years. And he was behind schedule—yeah, if nothing had completely actualized before thirty. At least, it was the last round up of the manifestation years. When his request should be considered at long-run. Nothing had reminded him he was behindhand but this controversial pregnancy. None of his unyielding efforts towards his dream about authoring worldwide top-rated books, and making pot of money from them, had half reminded him he was lacking behind in manifestation—really. Maybe if this debatable pregnancy wasn't raising ugly head, it would have been the inspiring mark of accomplishment.

He waited and fantasized that noble fulfilment before thirty, when even if a pot of wealth didn't come along, he had an envious home—a beautiful wife worth of pride—a child probably a son, and then children. Maybe he got a neat lucrative job to crown them. The divine intervention? The answer to his age-long prayers? Could it be them—sure? And this controversial incident a miracle? But he was too sceptic that the emergent miracle was losing its substance the way it crept in. The inspiring thought got weaker and weaker and flatter and flatter that before he realized it the ungovernable pessimism was wearing it out. With one abrupt thrust of his thoughts, he shoved the dwindling dregs, asking himself what kind of Band-Aid he would term that. Fallacy, hocus pocus or maybe sophistry.

When he alighted from the bus, a lovely sister was approaching to enter. "Mister Wyi Worri," she said. "You're a bit early to home today. In fact, I was just going to Akungba and thought I'd visit you in school." She smiled. "You know, you have a friend who's proud to tell your colleagues you're a sweetheart."

The congenial sister was a Yoruba and a neighbour, one of the few good ladies. Her family name was Iyebiye, and she was christened *Chrisette*. She was also a nurse. Her free close relationship was one he had hunted and craved for. She liked him but would want it greeting acquaintanceship. Not until she had unexpected heartbreak from her lover. It was too despairing and the misery seemed unbearable with incessant river-flow of her eyes. Now this sympathetic fragile condition gave Mr. Wyi Worri unexpected chance to bring her closer in his friendship. Advocating euphonious amity with his exploitative empathy of many facets and values he could manipulate with. Ranging from leering attention to bantering words of confabulation.

He would have loved to stay and talk, or even go back with her and brag a little, but he was really not in the mood. "That's good of you, sweetheart." He liked this sister; she was what co-dependent partner was all about—some stuff that was willing to give all. Her all. "Let me tell us the way it seems now, the stimulating love of he is winning the game."

Swaggering along the street of fawning villagers, he wondered how many admiring eyes had idolized him particularly, and then he had to walk the way back from school every day. He wasn't exactly associating their courteous idolatry with the obscene habit of ogling. No. If every other one who was a corps member with high regard NYSC government uniform, could get the same fashion of admiration, they could watch him anyhow they damn well pleased. He was a proud precious son of his country. An expensive graduate serving his country on an envious one year national service. There had to be some fringe benefits.

He got home and took his handset again, wondering this one he was calling again with his own line if she would pick. But she had to. Because the doctor in the General Hospital early hours of Monday, that twelfth January, said something about the ailment that actually tried to block her heartbeat Sunday night. It was Prince Williams that alerted the entire lodge, and the corps members carried her deadweight to the hospital. "It's… it's… just kind of bent of nature about the doctor's clairvoyance," he spluttered.

MyAngel didn't just start talking. She took her time. A longwinded time that was only an exacerbated suspended animation. Yeah, to Mr. Wyi Worri. At last she started plaintively; (I'll tell you what; men are a confused bunch… Accept his gifts, he thinks you're a gold digger… Refuse his gifts, he thinks you're playing hard to get… But give without demanding, he thinks you're a fool… Smile at him, he thinks you love him… Then let him kiss you and make love to you, he thinks you're cheap… Accept his love still, or act passionately, he thinks you're kinky or anyone else can have you… Uh-huh, combine him with others, he thinks you're insatiable… Become too…)

"Lady, don't forget, the doctor's suspicion is kind of propped up my misgivings…" he tried to cut her.

(Wait a minute…) she mercilessly went on. (Become too understanding, he takes you for a ride… and confront him with the truth, he thinks you're being bitchy…)

"I was just trying to remind you that the doctor's suggestion, after all, shored up my…" he started again.

(Mister Wyi Worri,) she stopped him rudely again. (Men are

14

this confused bunch, and you're not exempted... you're, in fact, the worst... the blossom worst!) She cussed and cut that line that way again.

Chapter Two

*H*e had a knock and tried to repress his frustration.

Miss Iyebiye, the sister he met on his way back from school, entered and was unaccustomed almost. She freely lay on his bed and was even schmoozing how his room was unkempt and needed urgent attention. Anyway, she volunteered to wash the dirty bed sheet covering the only comfort furniture in the room—except the wooden back-chair at his reading table.

"God knows how much ages you've worn that." She jeered at the small short he was wearing on. "Dirty boy," she joked.

But that satirical camaraderie wasn't what Mr. Wyi Worri needed. He wondered with some spasm of pity if Miss Iyebiye realized how deeply he cared about his love to MyAngel—even as the costly lover gave him unedifying brush off that deprived him of some look in; aye, some extenuating reasons for his baleful doubts. Nevertheless, he moved to her; very close that her face was inches from his. Then he drew her suddenly and kissed her lips.

"Oh!" she breathed.

"And that's a pleasant one?" he said daringly.

"I know you're not indirectly pressurizing me for sex?" she

rather accused.

"But if you're going to love me, Chrisette, you're going to do it." He tried her exorbitantly.

"The wisdom of relationship is first of all chaste," she pointed.

Of course that was a situation congenial to the expression of his self-restraint, but he insisted; "Still we're going to need to take it to some next level."

"Anyway, they're all manipulative lines men use to pressurize ladies into having illicit sex."

Impractical almost. Yeah, when he thought of his on-ground case with his fiancée. "Then you'll need a relationship that is morally clean and respects your envious chaste sexual boundaries."

"Of course, I won't settle for anything less!"

Gawd damned him for not settling right with stuff like this good sister! Was his sincere effort to have a worthy relationship failing again? But *Omni*, it was unfair! This was the second of his miserable snafu, and compellingly his mind dragged him to some wrench of fiasco of love he had been subjected to. There had been something about her—something about this paramour of torture of love that was real different from any other. And he had believed on her dangerously.

Aye, the miserable tears had come when he had to face the truth that he would never see to it he married this lady he had so much loved. Her love was such redemptive love that he had lamented if nothing could be rescued from the wrecked of his dream. He had really known what struck was gruesome, because his heart was grievously bartered. Yeah, for this Lady Telma, he had riskily accepted the loss of everything—

Maybe Mr. Wyi Worri knew what to do now. Maybe this was what he had to do now—leave this sister here to go on tiding the room, and find some spot. Some palliative rollicking spot.

*E*n route to Akure, he had allowed one cyclic thing. His troubled mind occupied it. It was the sorrowful mistakes of his youthful mischiefs. Like the mistake done to the intimate promise rendered to a tender heart of a defenceless sister. Her name was Jenifa, and she was a school girl who was his buddy. He had offered himself to her the day he still lost her. The unbelievable day she was expensively the fairy god-mother to his plight with the school authority. It was actually a touching issue of loss of a caring saviour of the day and tender love of the moonlight night.

Of course, moonlight night of sacrosanct promises. Inviolable promises not to be forgotten. But God should plead his case, there were mitigating circumstances like he was only thirteen and had lost her to far away town for years.

Then Madonna came up—and she was cutesy and loved him dearly. But they had to part their ways when they graduated from the school that brought them together.

Jenifa was still nowhere to be traced, so Madonna had self-appointedly come into the scene again. But now she was a chancer, and this and other things lost him his humanitarian conscience about making her a miserable antagonist to another sister he used to call Franz. Franciska was so fetching but had deadpan attitude about boyfriendship because of her unsophisticated view about love and sex. But beyond her power, and against her ethics, Franciska fell in love with him and realized that she had all along loved him to take her there. Yeah, she had needed him for her well-preserved pricey virginity. He was highly worth it maybe, as he himself was yet to experience canal knowledge.

Franciska was Madonna's significant rival, and though Madonna had unbeatable qualities, all he had cared was Franz was equally graceful. She loved him and he knew she would make a good wife. He measured the magnitude of his involvement into their relationship, it was a hell of a noose around his neck, yet he promised and kept her believing with every wish he would keep up to it.

But did he actually? Another one, Chrixtabel, had distracted and disrupted this sincere pledge. She was the fanciable lady he met en route to Ibadan for his O' level exams. She was the strange lady that had sprouted his natural tendency to begin behaving in a particular way about her—with that sense of déjà vu that really gave him madness calculating. She was discreet and reserved and sensible, because she was as much mysteriously phony.

Meanwhile, when they alighted at the terminal park, he had followed her in order to break her complication—and she was less enamoured with him pestering and tracing her. And she was going to charge him for stalking, and even signed the pledge of hitting his face as deterrence. Anyway, cupid—the god of love— favoured him and brought the opportunity he kissed her soft lips under happy circumstance.

But that wasn't enough. He traced her to that emporium he got the address. And she took him to an inn where she had wanted to explain that which he didn't know about her, and needed to know and be on a safe side about her love—But her excessive gratuitous jealous references to his past, and coupled with her undue hardboiled slow pace in jettison her convoluted phony life, made him to find her intolerably obdurate—and he critically had it in his way, which was *case closed*.

Well, he said Chrixtabel was mysteriously phony—and she was transcendentally. She was Chrixtabel by name but *gracious Gawd*, he found out incidentally she was Jenifa!

Jenifa—the tender school girl of sacred promises he had violated.

Chapter *Three*

*I*t was around seven post meridian, and this section of casino was with rip-roaring revelry. It was a long hall that filled to capacity with trendy carousers, and before he would wonder a little bit longer, he had known why more than half of these bustle and hustle people were on suits. Suit was a welcomed modern befitting dressing culture in Africa, for both men and women alike, for marriage ceremony. The entertainment had claimed the room not just for the gay item 7, but for showcasing female and male versions of classy suits.

The atmosphere was straight out of having everything doing with shindig. Everyone was letting out loud guffaws as if in competition for who would become hysterical with ballyhoo. Mr. Wyi Worri took a seat at a table near the exit door, the only vacant place he scanned easily. It was some furniture with ritzy embroidery of shiny filigree, the kind used by avaricious racketeers, as they crossed their legs gazing at their glasses of rich wine. Anyway, this was Akure, the capital city of Ondo state, and commissioners had their occasions and merriment with all these luxuries deposited by the government.

Mr. Wyi Worri was watching admiringly at a young man

running his fingers around the rim of his wine glass, playing along while he smiled lustfully into his lady's face.

No; Mr. Wyi Worri was rather watching admiringly at the lady, the partner in question, with a very big implacable sense of déjà vu. Incomprehensibly. So fondly familiar, as if stirring something inside him. When she tried to smile at him, it was well-disposed, but he didn't wait to absorb that. He averted his face.

He was watching the meritorious merrymaking for another moment, when another sister came up to his table and poured wine into two glasses. She was very beautiful and fair in complexion that he doubted she was a Yoruba too. Yeah, fair and beautiful, pleasing to the eye. She dressed in regalia of a tailored pin-striped shirt that blended decorously with green skirt and tie. If he would just stand up, she would no doubt tower over him.

"You're our guest, you know," she said to Mr. Wyi Worri. "Even if you're a stranger and a tourist."

"I'm not, right; at least I don't hang… or look lost. Do you know how wrongly that compliment came?"

"I know how repellent it makes you look." She pulled out a chair, losing her tie and smiling at him. "Like an also-ran, who feels this prosaic lady has just started this very awkwardly." She sat and relaxed, unbuttoning her shirt to reveal her tantalizing pale skin. "Like a no-hoper, who feels this lady just started this on a very bland platform that'll leave his fantasies floundering helplessly."

Mr. Wyi Worri tipped his glass and let the drink slid down his throat hungrily. "My killer's with theatricality rather. She's Freudian. Maybe my type so appreciate her. Of course, all the real guys understand them. So what's the deal with this flirtation?" He grinned.

"At first I wasn't intending some coquetry, but the lustful fine boy was disappointed… reminding me what I so much love to do. You know, I love to flirt over men that look good… men with this kind of roving eyes you have here." She smiled and it was highly coquettish.

21

"I understand; men of fancy free… like little randyness in this type of gay hurly burly."

"You're worldly," the hostess accused. "If you're kind of lucky about my dalliance… maybe I want to handle another handsome guy to his real fantasy… I'll be all in for you."

"Of course, you throw it all on me, as if it's outpouring!" he wondered rather.

"You know it…" she laughed; "like sexual theatrics."

"No, I don't really know it; I'm serious, girl. They jeopardize my ethics."

"Huh?" she dismissed that.

"Now…" he looked up; "watch these snazzy sisters hanging around these men."

"What's the big deal about the ladies?"

"They depict prostitutes soliciting openly, with those worldly clothes."

"Do you mean something like this?" she pointed; "Speechless."

"That's the name?" he said, wondering.

"Fashion statement. This is a gay party; it can't be all that bad."

"Let me tell you something; you call it *'Speechless'* because people are still in shock and ashamed on their behalf. It's not just the gay party. Of course, they're caught in public buses wearing open shoulders with visible heads of breasts, and their outfits are quite offensive."

"Nice man; reminds me of my ex sometime. He was a good decent man. I fell in love with him, but it didn't bring joy to my life. I actually hated myself, because I fall easily for men with good minds," she said retrospectively.

A male attendant was crossing with bottles of chilled beer; Mr. Wyi Worri waved him. "Even when you have a body as hot as the body of Sharon Stone, it's still good to keep some part covered in public," he continued, ignoring her nostalgic retrospection. "Okay… look at this old woman…" he threw his face to a middle aged lady, who was wearing a thin skirt that was cut up the hip, exposing her body pruriently. "This is abomination! *Omni Heaven*, when they say keep it covered, they're not saying that it should be kept covered with this short flimsy fabric." He shook his head with disapproval, and before he could stop himself he had shouted; "Woeful! For crying out loud, her G-string is visible!"

"You're shouting," the girl cautioned him strangely.

"So what's that desperate act about?"

"Uh-oh! Do you worry in the world we are now, what people do with their clothe line in some hedonistic mirth like this?" She was, of course, surprised. "She's simply a sex bomb with her trend-setting outfit."

"*Gawd*, girl, she just assaulted the spirit of my Jury; it couldn't help feeling pity," he besmirched that opinion. "Is it actually imaginable that a woman of her age is wearing this in a public gathering? Of course, this is contrary to some section of dress code of my jury style addict. She's to be sentenced thereby to life strictly in Sharia community. She's to be restricted to practical Muslim areas. Tout court!"

"Tout court?" she inquired.

"Shekinah," he answered.

"Well, I don't care where you think she'd be sentenced to; all I know she's one real chic fetching lady. What she needs is some good booze-up, a virile lover… or both. That's what I think. You know, good fuck is better when you're a bit drunk. She's going to drive men crazy with that smashing dressing style. It's hot, mark my word."

"Yeah, hot and sleazy." He was glaring at this loony partner of his in a new fashion, like seeming manners.

"Sounds like a pot calling the kettle black, Reverend Thomas Aquinas." She turned her head, but then faced him again. "Take a big slug of that drink and feel horny and ensconce yourself." She pouted invitingly, but whispered; "Your Lady, Miss Togbe, will be available soon."

"My lady, Miss Togbe?" he said incredibly. It was over seven years now he had last heard of any Miss Togbe.

'Kemi', he heard a woman's voice calling the lady, and she stood rather.

The hall was obstreperous and bustling, and his ears were adjusting to the rummage of that voice or the owner. His eyes followed the lady attendant, but another tempting lady hostess tried to stop her.

'Bee ni, I've welcomed him as an honoured guest' he heard the first hostess shout to this another lady.

They could be referring him, but he was scanning the hall for the first voice. He was almost sure it belonged to that first sister that tried to lure his attention with some warm-hearted smiles. Maybe she was this lady that wanted him honoured guest. But for what free benevolence? From the look of things, the entire classy hussies and half the rakes in this town were here. He rarely visited this kind of resort, or this kind of all night long party. There wasn't in all his life he could remember, enough time for his writing; and if not his niggle doubts at hand, socializing with such level of liberated people wasn't his strong suit.

Meanwhile, the Miss Togbe he knew was a damsel in distress her motorcycle conked out; the stranded NYSC copper he met years back as he rounded that traffic circle. He was actually trekking down town on that deserted road to thumb a car. She was voluptuously robust, and had a beautiful face. And he had instantly adored her full-round head of hairs. And under that terrible heat of the sun he had helped her clean her oil-soaked plug that she promised him some kindness in a special way.

Presently, that another lady attendant came up to his table. "Hey, sir, you're one of the guests of honour tonight; what's your pleasure?" She started hoisting a brand of beer from the serving basket; "I guess Gulder is okay?"

"Yeah... thanks." Gulder was the brand he just took.

"And um... sir, some food?"

"No, sweetheart... thanks." He didn't feel like eating.

"You're welcome." She exhibited some warm smiles.

She was moving away when he flagged her and added impulsively; "Maybe you order some more bottles of beer for me." ...Yeah, might as well do it right, he thought. That was exactly what guys usually did when they had a bad time—come over some place like this and get smashed. It had appeared not to work for him, but this time it had to offer the presence of mind needed.

Today was a rough one to his trained mind, and the dirty trick—the questionable bun in the oven—was weighing heavily on it.

"*Whoa*, I'm impressed!" The first fair skinned waitress returned, and was all smiles. "Maybe…" she continued, as what she was getting from Mr. Wyi Worri was a level stare; "I'm not really. I and Miss Togbe were just talking about you."

"Miss Togbe?" he intoned. *So Miss Togbe was really that first lady sitting with that man!*

"She's the younger sister to the celebrant."

"Yeahhh," he intoned, still in daze.

"Yes, she just told me how warm-hearted she was about having your relationship; but guess, you were not positive. You walked away," she chortled.

Aye, she laughed but that really wasn't funny. Adverse emergency like resurfaced Miss Togbe presented another problem Mr. Wyi Worri had to slug out—a new breakneck problem brought on again by the creepy fate. Now he had to face the salacious brazen deviation he had been dazzled with— some warmth of her provocative friendship with far more palpable sexuality and much formidable driving force. It wasn't going to be easy. Yeah, as it had seemed this kind of dangerous temptation had become his immutable phenomenon.

Miss Togbe had wanted him to believe one true fact about the double-life of Mabel, his then girlfriend—it was true he said he met her an NYSC copper on the way and had helped her, but at the end of the day she didn't take him along, as she had heavy luggage riding together with her. Then she knew she owed him some favour in a special way—Aye, if they met again.

And of course they met in a school she was doing her primary assignment as a teacher, and which he had come to re-sit for his O'level examination. She had called him in her room to send home this substantive information about his girl, as a temptress. A temptress with high sense of seduction, because she had let him visit her when she just took her bath and was massaging her nude body in some slow romantic pace. And *strewth!* she didn't mind his voyeuristic interest, making him a poor Peeping Tom. Sensual confusion had clouded his system, that he had wondered what he fatefully walked into. He knew it was a crafty trick to seduce him to suffocation without substantive motive.

Presently, Mr. Wyi Worri lifted his face; unbelievably Miss Togbe was standing a few tables over, discussing with an attendant. Bossy. Then she sashayed to the table just behind the sister sitting with him. She was greeting the couple of that table with every sensational smile. She had that air that carried excitement enticement. A trait that was beguilingly visible in her ever-present sexuality theme. Miss Togbe remained a sex bomb to his senses no doubt.

Mr. Wyi Worri tried to look back into the servile eyes of the sister sitting there with him; "I guess, you transferred my playing-hard-to-get to logical conclusion of me being sexually hard-boiled? But, at least, you appreciate my continence; right?" His eyes were supposed to burn into this sister's lustre, but they were willing him to turn them up again. Instead of succumbing to that cheap failing, he took the sister's hand. "At least, you were impressed by that bottled-up sexual repertoire, huh?"

"For your mind," she smiled mildly, then added; "do you think so?"

Now he heard a sensational high laugh of a sister, who he was certain was Miss Togbe, and automatic pause was felt along his sensuality. But then the laughter was lost in the hysteria background, and he didn't lift his eyes.

"She's trying your cool," the sister said, knowing Mr. Wyi Worri was feeling nervous as Miss Togbe made most of her moment. "But she's just coming to meet you."

That last sentence hoisted Mr. Wyi Worri's face. Now trapping of glamour. Miss Togbe's cream colour suit wasn't only special designer, but her plated pair of shoes. She had expensive looking pieces of jewellery around her necklines and wrists. It was an open top that was complimented with open neck black tight underwear, gypsy skirt, and long hosiery of net black sucks that started from the loin and trailed down the lovely legs.

"I guess you call me crazy!" Miss Togbe said at last, placing her glass on the table.

Her words once again turned his thoughts to the danger she posed. For the past two years he was sober to trade with caution in the tiger's lair, couching his mind, not just it, his wayward limber system, to uphold the obligation of having regard to the pre-nuptial vow he took. There was no need to join the fire brigade to put out fire, since he was wearing grasses around his waist. MyAngel was all a man, particularly he, would want in a woman. Splendour. To start with, she was fair in completion, having the colour proximate to the American white, which was his madcap choice. She again flaunted a height that was most commensurate with his average height of five feet five. She was voluptuous, which complimented his trim pale body. Her dressing line wasn't just elegant, but had the touch of panache. Her face carried the overall eye-opener. Her walk was queenly— as if she knew that only her for him deserved that air of confidence of perfection.

Perfection? Spotless then? He wasn't so sure now. The fact that she might have violated the sacred regard attached to the dignity of vow of their betrothal. And maybe this was what sent him to neurosis, that he wouldn't possibly tolerate any misconduct on the ground of infidelity, and with such magnitude of flippancy. That was the ugly part of a woman a man, particularly he, wouldn't want.

Miss Togbe moved to sit where the other sister sat, and she unseated her. "She's a friend; a good friend," she said to that dramatic obeisance.

Mr. Wyi Worri saw the sister heading in her way and fading in the jolly party. Another one approached with a bottle of wine, lifted new glasses and looked at Miss Togbe. She nodded a go-ahead order. Then he saw Miss Togbe lifting two glasses for him to take one. He was better confused.

"Yours for blissful cheers," she said. "For our reunion, right?"

"No... yeah, I mean... no..." he even blushed; he was

puttering like a coward. Miss Togbe was doing him this. But he had never been cowardly in her face. "I was actually saying," he continued; "it's been like those days I had the effrontery to walk away." Aye, he had actually walked out on her like the fair sister had tried to detract him. He had done that nobly, and it didn't again allow bonafides to believe on what he should have safely believed on the snapshot about his girl. "Arrogant; isn't it?" He lifted a corner of his mouth, which produced a likable slight grin. "Was it really that presumptuous?"

"No, you were inimitable cracker jack," she giggled. "It was inviolate rather."

"Well, I still don't mean it contemptuous now I refuse to take this wine; I was taking beer already."

"I understand…" she smiled; "the fine boy wouldn't look like he drinks gluttonously."

"That's the problem," he conceded, suspecting her a bit drunk than he himself was now.

"No problem," she laughed again; it was the same hysterical giggles. "Take your cup of beer, it's allowed. I know that my goodness and love will be with you all your life, and my house will be your home as long as you live." She raised her cup.

Mr. Wyi Worri didn't raise his cup, but said, prevaricating; "Nice recitation there." He clapped lightly. "You read psalms, amazed; you and holy bible!"

"You, nicely parried." She raised her cup again, urging him to do the same. "Now, are we good to go?"

"No." He still didn't fall in with the idea. "The fact that you desired to lure your student, and was actually out in that room to seduce him into having affair with you, makes me sick to think what you're capable of doing now it seems somewhat right under the influence of gay party. Such cheers of reunion are just something I don't get used to."

She hunched forward over the table that she was so near. Now their faces lay, their lips were touching. She felt Mr. Wyi Worri swallow nervously, but didn't see him backing out like she was a snake, she said; "You actually remember the last time we were both in my room? I do." She allowed a little space between them in case he belched. "You were watching my breasts hungrily. You couldn't withdraw your gaze; you were nothing near abashed nor embarrassed. You know, your eyes were lustful and full of that particular emotion. You know, all the way down your loin was fire. You wanted it... you watched my body hungrily. I caught you in fragrante, remember!"

"My last time in your room was actually designed for your convenience... to get me fallen in with your enchantment... and was over six years ago. Miss Togbe, if my memory serves us well, you were like a shameless she-goat on heat, and you were deceitful. You were all this just to your student."

"At least I wasn't an opportunist, you know, Mister Wyi Worri. Though you were my student, we were at the same age bracket." She moved close again, looking into his eyes. He refused to look away, allowing her search them. She wasn't even hurt as she was there prying where she didn't really belong. And she might even try to kiss those lips.

Any animal with a long tail should never attempt to jump over a bonfire, Mr. Wyi Worri quickly stood up. This was too daring. It wasn't a congenial situation to brave his self-restraint. "I need to go outside, God knows." He turned to head for the exit door, then shouted over his shoulder; "And I never in my life, as those days lasted, had sexual urge, as part of my repertoire, with any sister aside my girlfriend... not even that Mabel you knew, but franz, the one you didn't know!"

There were a lot of things Mr. Wyi Worri had never wished he would ever stop to do; things far more sterling and commendable than having controllable sexual urge for his teacher. One of them was having inspiring resolution against having indulgence outside his fiancée. Although he was accusing MyAngel of cheating behind him, he had remained faithful and chaste despite the sexless months of unavoidable respite caused by the distance of their stations.

Moving away from that section, he knew he had nowhere to rest his head. And some noises from another casino were only inviting jollity.

Chapter*Four*

*I*n a minute his sight was smothered with mental obscenities unimaginable. It was another raunchy scene—greater raunchy scene of high spirit and jollity. Involuntarily, an unusual feeling was there again. Running through his spine. His mind was between two options. Should he brave it and watch the mental poison or show his back swiftly to the seamy scene, to preserve his already derelict sense of decency. Reluctantly, he didn't leave. He rather pushed inside.

This particular pub knew what it means to define orgiastic atmosphere. Bawdy lyrics were pumping out in funkiness of heating air. Sounds of laughter. Dancing randy nude ladies swift to and fro. They were endowed with right portions of flesh at the right places that one couldn't do anything but touched to have a feel of them. *Gawd, that's sexual harassment—stop it!*

Though he stood with indignation at the vulgarity that popped up with real warning, he marvelled at his lukewarm decision on not showing his back instead. Where were all his spiritual evolution and reasons put there by the Catholic dogmas? And he desired to stay on the indecency, which he knew the extent it was tantamount to open debauchery?

Now he noticed a group of men on their own almost. They rounded this table with their drinks as if they were on some meeting.

"Do you know that the supreme pontiff went to United Kingdom to be welcomed by Queen Elizabeth two, in the first visit of pontiff to the country in almost thirty years, and met hostile welcome?"The speaker with the group said. "I'm saying number one representative of son of God has his visit marked with symbolically hostile significance!" The speaker shuddered unbelievably.

"You see it, brothers." Another one grinned stupidly, looking about to feel every attention given to him. "You see it," he repeated pugnaciously—still allowing the daft grin on his face. "He said Pope Benedict the sixteen's trip to UK was welcomed with questionable mixed feeling by the Queen, why? Because we're in a changing world, and mustn't weigh every changing social matter with inimitable spiritual measure."

"But that should be a contorted version of the truth in that caustic story!" another talker wondered. "First importantly, your description is wholly uncompendious. If there was any true hostility, the Queen didn't show it. The trip was surely the first state visit by a pope to UK, but by and large, his meeting with the Queen was symbolically significant because of the historical divide between the officially protestant nation and the Catholic Church. The Queen warmly welcomed him, and the Pope appreciated it as he recalled how Britain stood against Nazi Tyranny that wished to eradicate God from the society."

"Okay, you're right there…" The first talker responded counteractively; "not the Queen, but the British media was this particularly hostile to the Pope's visit."

"Friends," the second talker called up again. "Willy nilly you believe, the Queen is only there for the public, and this public expressed rejection; what are we talking again?" He showed the foolish grin—but not exactly, they had been somewhat alcoholic. "I read it myself equally. Protests were planned, and *Pope Nope* T shirt were spotted around London; all for what then?"

"Because," the third talker started readily; "they noted twelve million pounds security costed to tax payers at a time of austerity measure and job losses."

"Not really... not really..." the first talker was shouting; "it's largely because they strongly opposed to Pope Benedict's hard-line against homosexuality and particularly abortion, and the use of condoms to prevent AIDS spread. But these are essential for the changing ethics of the changing world, with the changing time."

"I know I'm a stinking sinner but if you ask me, I'll say I give kudos to Pope. That's pure sanity... restoring dignity of divine Christianity honestly, and without bias, fear or favour. The hearts of men are fully set to do evils, if otherwise." The third talker grinned, leering tightly.

But it seemed all of them here were heavily tipsy; Mr. Wyi Worri nevertheless found himself having delectation to settle within the group.

"Sure, the hearts of men born of women are full of quirky evils," A new talker was coming in; "This papacy we're talking about here controls and influences half people of this world, any mistake from him towards this particular sensitive talk of abortion, half of the world is extravagantly misled. After all..." he eyed the second talker and challenged; "what if you were aborted, you'd have been denied the world. Alright..." he was challenging again; "what if Mandela was aborted? Eclipse of Apartheid would've persisted in the buttocks of Africa."

They all laughed like drunks they were; but these arguments from these intoxicated drunks were not just informative, they were interesting. Mr. Wyi Worri found a seat within them.

"Of course, what if Jenner and Ross, Fleming and Koch were aborted, leprosy and malaria infections and TB would still be mysteries today." Another talker even stood and contributed—leering sluggishly.

Mr. Wyi Worri watched this man with a peculiar interest. No doubt, this man was suffering the dreaded disease of TB—or maybe—no doubt, this convalescent had suffered the dreaded disease of TB, because he was as thin as someone who the dreaded cough had viciously taken his flesh.

But everybody was nursing his drink except Mr. Wyi Worri. He stood again, and was shuffling out to get his own bottle. The noise from this side was deafening, but he pushed to pull any waiter. The stage was now cleared of the abominable sight of the dancing damsel, but not cleared of bawdiness. He watched the wild manic musician on the podium, and even tempted to move back and shout at the group as his contribution; *What if*, who did he want to mention, Lucky Dube? Ok, *Jimmy Cliff was aborted, reggae would've remained with sad knowledge that this excellent type of music could only be performed in a rumbling of drunks and lunatics and psychopaths in dreadlocks and the heck of it, propelled by Indian hemp… like this lunatic on the stage!*

However, Mr. Wyi Worri was retracing to the group. He had to make his own contribution and fast—Knowledge of God as bedrock was what everybody should put at the back of their minds. Someone was contributing;-

"What if Michael Jackson was aborted… the magic Michael Jackson…the flexible body of songs and dance… celestial Michael Jackson… Lord, it'd have been loss upon loss!"

It was the third talker who contributed. Michael Jackson of USA, the legendary music maestro, the electrifying musician, was who he was talking with that brazen high sense of hero-worship. Eulogy. Nonetheless, may his soul rest in peace—Mr. Wyi Worri prayed and waited.

"What if Mohammed Ali was aborted, the feat of Negroid-Caucasians would've still been in doubt, and Luck Marciano White noise unending."

Oh, this one was great! It was done with every bit of pan-Africanism, which Mr. Wyi Worri was proudly part of. Mohammed Ali, the great black man boxer—the legend of his time. Anyway, he waited still.

"What if Messi was aborted, the Spanish-Argentina wizard, this man of soccer impossibilities would've been denied the world."

Messi—*the football merciless Messi,* Mr. Wyi Worri even thought that with some sense of admiration; the La-liga mystery. Okay, now he was going to talk his own. He wouldn't sit down. He stood and didn't hesitate to put across his own foolish alcoholic grin. "What if Jesus was aborted by Mary and Joseph, being a child of hapless circumstance..." he paused, for the sudden attention that was given to him was rather strange. He grinned again, but continued in a sober voice; "Yeah, brothers, he was a transcendental burden... Jesus was to his parents. I mean, like a strange cross planted on the shoulders of a teenage virgin betrothed to an unusual man. The gospel surely, would've been washed into the drains with him, and worse, brothers..." he shouted over their prosaic cooperation; "the human captivity by Satan would've remained permanent! Man would've lost and become completely barbaric... and then Thomas Hobbes' derision in grave would've been eternal." He leered defiantly at them. "Do you understand what I mean?" He was no doubt drunk himself. "I mean survival of the fittest!" He shouted at the anti-climax—the non-event—accorded to his dear contribution.

But they were laughing at him. Aye, he was their source of hilarity. They were enjoying his banana skin; but how he wished these young men here knew it was love really that wrong-footed him, and gave them that derisive right to sully his contribution. "Yeah, you laughed at that unusual input, but lack of fear of God is behind these loopholes in the eternal verity." Mr. Wyi Worri watched them lugubriously. "They say love is precious and answereth all things, but you don't have to believe anymore," he continued non-sequitur; "We hear love is beautiful like a butterfly... yeah, butterfly; the more you chase it the more it eludes you. It hurts... it never makes you happy like they say." He saw himself taking them more the wrong way. "You laughed at me, but brothers, I tell you, there's no one again to be worth special love. Take your time to choose and still it's difficult to get the best... Guuuuush!" He hissed and walked away, shoulders hung in despair. No one should have said *'I love you'* if they didn't mean it! No one should have talked about feelings if they were not there! No one should have *Gawd*, touched a life if they meant to break a heart! No one, God knows, should have, for the heck of it, looked in the eyes of another, when all they did was lies! The cruellest thing one could do to another was to let them fall in love, when they didn't intend to catch them… and this should go to his girl, MyAngel. Tout court.

A man in the group followed him outside, the guy with that sense of pan-Africanism, and he gave him ears as he called him aside.

Without introducing himself, the man started; "Let me tell you what that blind black man with incredible vision said. He's a pop musician from USA, the Gods own country. You know him?"

"Yeah," Mr. Wyi Worri was impatient; "Steven Wonder."

"Right man. That Steven Wonder really wonderfully let the world know that vision is more than eyesight. And it's more than hindsight. It's really beyond insight. And it's still more than foresight. In situ, it has phenomenal high powered unstoppable destination… not just definition; do you get?"

"Yeah, sir," Mr. Wyi Worri said.

"Now," the man was saying again; "this man of extraordinary, in his preaching he titled *'so what the fuss'*…"

"Sir, you're talking about his music; I don't know him as a preacher," Mr. Wyi Worri cut the man.

"Right, man," the man said. "In this music he featured Prince En Vogue, he says, *'this man, if you're locked in a marriage and your other half just gives you abuse, yet you've convinced yourself that there's no way out, shame on you'*. Man, if you go home now, like an African child who suckled his mother's breast well, count your teeth with your tongue sensibly. This mood you're, everybody knows damn well, could cost you your life… and if *'yet you keep doing what you should do without, shame on you'*. I think," he grinned admonishingly; "this Steven Wonder man adds something like that." He touched Mr. Wyi Worri's shoulder. "I always tell my friends who're *'still holding on'*, a sad thing about life is when you meet someone and fall in love only to find out in the end that it's never meant to be, and that you've wasted years and effort on someone who's not worth it. If she's not worth it now, she's not going to worth it a year or ten years from now; let go." He watched the confused Mr. Wyi Worri a moment. "Now, the party's till dawn, come back to the table of men and merry away that hurtful load of the heart... at least this one night."

"Yeah, I will..." Mr. Wyi Worri agreed but added; "Just a second for a call, if you'll leave."

"No problem," the man said and left.

"*M*yAngel, it's me," Mr. Wyi Worri said into his device.

(Hold on, Mister Wyi Worri, let me bid a lovely night to my caller, who's on hold; you don't know him, anyway!) MyAngel replied.

Mr. Wyiwori thought it was insane for a lover to have a private caller, as well as rude impetus to keep her man waiting for the care of this caller, except for her pique on his rough justice on her.

(What do you want again?) She said at last.

Mr. Wyi Worri felt fear clutch at his heart—and the rudeness even caused his eyes gasp with shock. MyAngel was getting more implacable to wring his neck. Mr. Wyi Worri guessed what it was like to go through underserved wrongheaded accusation, and was however trying his best to let it slide—thinking it was just post-hoc reactional phase of ripple effect. "You were lying there exchanging banters on phone with those intruders, when you should reason with me on why I had to get the wrong end of the stick; where's your decent love?"

(The intruders care, if you don't know... and my decent love's rude, because unfairly it meets an awful appreciation.)

Mr. Wyi Worri pictured her there, as always, in nostalgia; this was, yeah, if he survived it, a one story in her ventured love life she would never forget. It was as much sorrow in his own soul.

But did he completely go wrong, with that alarm button he spearheaded? His game had been tight, and he had trusted her. Poor boy, he was! All the time it was for this pathetic trust. And this was just killing him to know that, maybe satisfactorily, she was sexually prone to affiliate with some other brother. *For the heck of it, Omni*, she shouldn't have done that!

"Tell them your true lover is not tired yet, and he can walk up to the moon and back to see he cares for you; and he'll just be happy and relaxed in a few explanations on your oestrus circle."

(Mister Wyi Worri, dates of my period are known to you, and of course, you should know sometimes predicting ovulation wouldn't be consistent… explain it yourself.)

"Anyway, I love you…" Mr. Wyiwori was whispering when the line got dead. He saw her proud face in his mind and tried to match it with her tone of voice. His own surviving angel, his precious possession of life-partner, was becoming more audacious and remorseless. He brought down his handset. Only a few weeks ago, MyAngel was lying on his bed there, awake in the night for hours, kinky and enthralled at every single love he passed to her. Now she hung up on him insupportably. If MyAngel had spoken that way to those interlopers, they would surely abandon her to suck her wound. But she said their loves were caring, and his was harmfully unappreciative. Well, modus operandi had it that each member of a round table partnership, like matrimony, had right to their feelings—MyAngel had right to talk back. And now Mr. Wyi Worri adored inalienable rights.

She should have been her Ladyship—her redoubtable Ladyship, he thought as he walked back to the mirth; shuddering abominably. She should have been a redoubtable Olympian feminist out of the top-drawer. Maybe a human right activist for complete emancipation of women—for girl-power.

MyAngel knew he said the truth, and cutting him out that way was a way to cover up. Let her tell him she was unfaithful to him, for that she was only releasing him to allow other ladies' love to himself, *because mouse that has two holes would not die easily*—he would believe her. But telling him she wasn't comfortable to be his wife anymore, because he had loved her, tolerated tormenting misery, and wanted her to have understandable heart to an innocent victim—he would not believe her.

<u>Chapter</u>*Five*

*T*his night had narcotic effect on Mr. Wyi Worri. Not because MyAngel was lying beside him—and not actually because he had taken any drug, or it was a case of narcosis. It was a case very equal but still obverse to narcolepsy. A condition in which he fell into slumber while his worrying suspicion highly raised the ugly head and aimed at his nerves…

*M*r. Wyi Worri wasn't feeling sceptic anymore. Just blissful prospects. Good and damned prospective.

The lady behind the counter was comely and fair complexioned. She smiled from ear to ear over his face. Her mouth pouting lovely, making her face take up with much sensation—and the huge lures of this attraction were so bewitching. He put them a serious check and went to sit down and wait, as she left to bring for him his stuff. Then he stood up again when she returned with a large heap of cards. At least, this heap would go round to every denizen of this country, who would care to attend his wedding ceremony. But who wouldn't care? Even his rivals?

Without a word but these charming smiles, she pushed the

cards she had wrapped into a pack across the counter. Then she picked one she missed, and was reading the inviting information.

She was very slow to look up and congratulate him, and it was necessary that he waited until she understood something there—because if she was thinking he had lost his heart to recognize those pleasing welcome smiles, he wanted her to know the tempting come-on was unnecessary and a wasteful effort. And he said at last;-

"I'm that Mister Wyi Worri, the soon April gentleman." He grinned unnecessarily. "And the lady, MyAngel, is my fiancée."

He drove down the streets, sharing out some cards to some couple of easily reachable friends.

Then he drove to tell his soon-to-be in-law, Frank Desmond, that marriage agreement had been made between him and their sister—and possibly let them have their own copies. But Mr. Wyi Worri's father ought to make this journey with him, to show the grounded support of the family! He pulled at the compound, but he didn't disembark immediately. He thought a little and opened his dashboard. Inside was an envelope that was addressed to him.

It read;-

Dear Son,

This letter is written to you that in the event of my withdrawal it is entirely likely I am inconvenienced, for I am solidly behind your manly decision. Somewhere around my twenty-four, my mannish race to matrimony had completed, and you know, around your age, I have got the first three of you. You will find the positive inspiration of my bold precocious step as an evidence of my total approval.

Dad

That was all there to it, but it was enough. Enough to convince his in-laws of his paternal blessing to himself and to their daughter. He stuck the expensive paper in his chest pocket and got down.

He knocked at the door; "Mister Wyi Worri, knocking."

"Mister Wyi Worri?"

"Uh-huh"

"Wait, somebody is coming."

But that voice looked like it was MyAngel's? When did she return? Better still, how did she return without letting him know? And they talked yesterday—and this morning too? He waited.

A couple of minutes, then some shuffle of feet, and Frank Desmond opened the door.

"Frank, I brought news for you."

"Maybe I have news for you, too," Frank Desmond sounded raw. "Why did you really come?"

"For you… your people, I must say."

"Your friend came home to make sure all the arrangement for her marriage is completely put in place. It's next week, and tonight's her hen-party night."

"Next week? No!" Mr. Wyi Worri wondered. "It's next month." He grinned to that mistake. "You see, that's why I came to correct this. She wouldn't know I've picked a date this coming month, and made these cards." He flipped out a good number of cards.

Frank Desmond watched the cards, he couldn't make out things. "For who?"

"For me and your sister, of course," he perplexed. "She may have not told you, but we have to be husband and wife. Of course, she returned for it?"

"No, not you. She came for a suitor, who has been taken these ceremonial steps for her hand in marriage."

The air couldn't find its way into his lungs. Frank Desmond's words were still there in his ears, and finally he got the horrible sense out of them. "She came home… for a proper arrangement of her trousseaux… to live with another brother, who has come for her hand in marriage?"

"Yeah. At least, that's the way I figure it," Frank Desmond said. "Mother thinks she's really happy and optimistic about her coming wedlock."

"She ought to be pregnant…" Mr. Wyi Worri started to say.

Frank Desmond cut him short; "Yeah. Mother smelled that too. There's this delicate way she holds herself, and mother asked and she admitted. Anyway, this suitor said it was him."

"Damn it, what about my own baby?"

Frank Desmond was obliging to explain. Too obliging. "My sister, MyAngel, is your sister, almost. If you were having romantic relationship we don't know. We only suspected and she didn't admit to us. This baby she's carrying is wholly for another man. It's only one pregnant for one man at a time... women know who truly father their babies. With boldness and enthusiasm, this suitor had said it was his. Period."

Mr. Wyi Worri's breath whistled out through his teeth. "When did this man come into marriage scene thing?"

"Evidently the time he came with full knowledge of her missing period," Frank Desmond said.

"The dowry?"

"Not yet. They're coming and going for the rigorous rites. He wants to finalize some other little little traditions, and then the full bride price will be negotiated and paid while the traditional wedding ceremony is going on. What do you think she didn't tell you, man, your mind is up to?" Frank Desmond said.

"I wish I know," he said. "I wish I know."

"There was this pathetic way she denied her affairs with you, I particularly observed... as if she'd have loved to involve you," Frank Desmond said.

Mr. Wyi Worri fished out the encouraging note. "Yeah, now I'm beginning to get it," he said, handing out the envelope to Frank Desmond. "My dad pleads his support here, and we'll be surely sooner ready to pay the bride price. This is the only way to fully own and monopolize a woman, and as you said he's yet to accomplish that."

"The pregnancy, remember brother!" Frank Desmond said.

"Damned... that's my pregnancy!"

"Maybe you'd like to tell me about it by her acceptance... but, brother, I tell you, that's a hell of double-booking!"

"We'll walk back to tell you. I'll have some time out with her." He started moving out.

"Good luck, Mister Wyi Worri," Frank Desmond said to that.

Mr. Wyi Worri walked into the short veranda and knocked at her door. Maybe his soon-to-be in-law, Frank Desmond, was wondering what his sister's style of transfer of child ownership would look like.

MyAngel's voice sounded inside; "Who's that... I'm busy."

Busy alone inside, he tried a grin. Unpleasantly. "I know you know it's me."

"Whatever, I think it's better you go away."

"It's just to have a word with you."

"No, thanks. I'm pretty busy."

"I'm leaving, beware."

"You have no choice."

"So"

"So that's that."

He shrugged sadly and dragged his feet back to Frank Desmond. He didn't talk immediately, but watched him dolefully.

Frank Desmond grinned and it was impish. "You didn't walk back to tell me," he said. "I hope to wait a long time."

"You'll help me get her out; do you mind, Frank? I really have to talk sense into this will-o-the-wisp sister of yours a second."

"Will-o-the-wisp!" Frank Desmond reminded him.

He nodded. "Pride. Besides, she got frozen out. I'd have trusted her a bit reasonably. Her love... her loveliness... all... would've been my sole and monopolistic possession. I like smart ladies."

"Her kind of smart?" Frank Desmond said.

"Especially. Will you help?"

"Maybe I was thinking this earlier, Mister Wyi Worri. I wanted to ask you if anything is felt of you, man, being all along in fools-paradise."

Mr. Wyi Worri's face faded. "I shouldn't answer you that, you know."

"But something is needed to answer here in this credulity."

"What? Ask me another thing you want and help me."

"Doesn't love actually sting? You know, people who play with it call it *game*, and some other thought these people irresponsible and call it *destiny*," Frank Desmond said. "You know, these second people really thought they understand

42

love… but perhaps they don't, at least they've realized it; haven't they?"

The imp came in Mr. Wyi Worri's eyes, and he truculently stood again. "They've not realized otherwise, I tell you. Love's still a destiny, and I've got this love and she's this love, believe me."

"Believe you other than the obvious… the stark reality… Mister Wyi Worri?" Frank Desmond stood as well. "You know something, some people who're wiser call this love *dream* rather, because it's like wild-goose chase, nobody truly has it."

"I said I have it, man, that pregnancy is mine! She's my destiny, I know!"

"Perhaps you still have time left for you to walk out and back again, and come up with proof, and I watch you do it now or anytime—" Frank Desmond tapped his shoulder; "Man, someday." He grinned snidely. "Good luck."

Mr. Wyi Worri stroked out his hand and swept out of the room—*if Frank Desmond doesn't know, even if his sister, the will-o-the-wisps, is truly having another man's pregnancy in lieu of his, it wasn't anything case of wild-goose chase or even fools-paradise—but Alice-in-wonder-land.*

"Do that!" Mr. Frank Desmond called behind him. "Then I'll let you teach me."

Now a maniacal simper followed.

*T*he horrible maelstrom woke him from the sleep; he jerked his body upright in his bed, feeling the apprehension and vagaries, and his psychopathology behind the creepy vision. MyAngel had actually double-dated, but he was relieved that it was a dream and not a proven earthbound fact yet. It was so psychic that it was almost quixotic. In his slumbers, he had been many adversarial things—done many conjugal things—and owned many up-market things, though this time around he was of prophetic pure reality happening almost. His eyes glued to the peacefully sleeping MyAngel, then he concluded it was only hallucination. Aye, a strange tremulous hallucination. And the next moment this *'strange'* about it made him shake the sedate lying lady.

"MyAngel! MyAngel!" he cried, big smothering jealousy choking his breath.

She moaned and turned over onto her side still asleep, her caring hand reaching out to him.

"Come on, wake up, MyAngel; I have this gloomy forecast you really have to start answering question about!" He said, beating off her hand, not really minding that brush off that prosaic way. "Wake up... come on!"

"Hu...hu, tomorrow morning," the sleepyhead whispered blearily. "Sweetheart...at dawn, please." That hand was now reaching for him again. "Come, let me hold you."

The entire coppers' lodge was empty, and MyAngel had visited this weekend. While every other clannish youth of this compound had used the mid-term break holiday to travel to their various needed places, Mr. Wyi Worri had stayed and invited her, because the sedate environment was dislodged of prying eyes in favour of the scandalous issue at hand. It was right on the connubial bliss, and there were a couple of things that really made high sense now around her controversial love. They looked good and attractive, and he gave them positive thought. One was this passionate way she made decision to keep his babe. Not many chic looking beautiful ladies would want a nebulous poor fellow put them into undignified motherhood.

There was another picture of her on the uncompromising track of matrimonial duty. A bigger wondrous commitment on this venture. The foetus since conception was a trouble, but the ambition to have his babe superseded—growing above it. Actually, it was malformed in the womb because of hormonal shortage, but she wouldn't for her immeasurable love get rid of it. And she had therefore resorted to manage it with medical prescriptions and advice. Now she had visited to let him feel her troubles with her, and then receive his Elysian sooths and love.

And that was when this nightmarish vicissitude—the bane of her conjugal inclination—started. Just today, the second day into her visit. She was coming out from the toilet on the left side of the door he seated watching about things, where she went to easy

44

herself, looking sepulchral.

He was instantly petrified and sprang to his feet. "What's the demon, MyAngel?" He pushed the panic button.

"Another problem," she bemoaned.

He moved close to her. "It's a bastard of a problem!"

He didn't mean to make it sound like it did. She looked hurt or maybe disappointed, but nevertheless nodded her head;

"I just started having bleeding." She watched his panicky movement to inspect on his own, and try to assuage that trepidation. "Oh, no need for that! You know, sweetheart, we'll take care of it."

He didn't sense otherwise and didn't mind to give any thought. Though it was true she came over for him to share real, and feel deep, her troubles—and this was the damnedest among, and she was too confident and resilient to do it off her own bait. He scrutinized the toilet some more, and felt her standing beside him. He grinned and she was relaxed. MyAngel was a poised okay chic. He pointed to the dent-less toilet. "You cleaned it so quick, and didn't call upon me?"

"Remarkable…huh?" She tried and did a trick with her mouth, and buoyant smiles smothered it. "I showed that bravery because I didn't want to shock you. It was a real gory sight."

"But you'd done beyond that with that kind of face you put outside there!"

This time she was hurt. Clearly. Not just disappointed. "You!" she said; it was soft, but it cracked like a plaint. It was painful plaintive self-pity, and her eyes were dark with distrust, and yet she didn't storm out. She stood there waiting for him to exercise the remaining in-grown repugnant instinct.

It didn't bother. "That's a lot of bravery… I mean, a silly lot of bravery, for a lady of clingy love!"

She watched him with some touching misery she gave in to. There were sudden tears in her eyes he wondered how the hell she took his little imprecation to let her know he needed her more closely, clingy and compatible. How indeed, she had to do that to herself!

"Oh, don't get sore at me!" He reached out and pulled her to himself, hiding his face in her ample bosom. She was pretty brave. "I don't mean to be a born lout, MyAngel. I so much pinned for true co-dependent clingy love, forgetting my manners. I should've appreciated the peerless bravery you put there for me."

She held his head—tilting it up until his face was aligned with hers. "For you, Mister Wyi Worri."

The sorrow around her eyes was all gone. Coming out of the glum was a new kind of luscious beauty. "I know quite well… and I love you, my lady."

She had let his lips come up to hers. "I love you, too," she said, her arms going around his shoulders. "Please, kiss me and assure me you won't be an ingrate over my love again."

Mr. Wyi Worri saw her lips quivering, and then let his hands go around her dutifully, and held her there until he finished assuring.

"Now did it help?"

She nodded, and there were tears in her eyes again.

"Stop, it's okay." He mopped her eyes with the back of his hand. "Please, stop." Then he gently led her back to the room where he would assure her better.

<u>Chapter</u> *Six*

*W*hat a horrible vision again, *Gawd!*

Mr. Wyiwori woke up and sat up, breathing rapidly. Horrified, yeah. He was blinking horribly. That was just what he could do now. There were times he thought himself a somnambulist—having companionship with Iris, the divine messenger of Morpheus. Times he knew he was a somniloquist; but like a mirage, there was no where he could find this goddess from the god of dream now.

*T*hey were having discussion on MyAngel's anomalies in love; it was in his room here, for there he sat by his table, putting down some report on MyAngel's case, and this goddess visited in the wraith of Chinonso—his cousin. But Chinonso was healthy and alive back there in the village, he thought, and she was heart and soul with her unalloyed support to his union with MyAngel?

Well, it was reality Chinonso's phantom was sitting at the head of his bed there facing him. She was whitish and was in a long white garment that connoted she visited for peace. It had been like horror-struck, and he had collapsed over the table, but she had helped him sit up again, and cuddled him until he was well and ready to start talking.

"Ah!" He ejaculated, shaking his head questionably, maybe to nullify the effect of the shock of some snapshot this phantom had just wanted him to believe. There was raw pain that greased over his feature, from where you could tell the drastic magnitude of this harrowing upset; but he wasn't holding it against Chinonso. After all, *spirits were inviolable.*

When he talked again, the doubt was obvious. "Where did you pick up this rough news?"

"Huh! Perhaps I'm feeding you with mere rumour? But spirits are infallible!"

"Yeah, I know; but why would you pick up this destabilizing information?"

"Have you ever thought you were a stopgap?"

He frowned at Chinonso's phantom uncomfortably. "If I was I don't remember it," he drawled. "But you talked her as past?"

This spirit laughed at him pitifully.

"You know what, sis? I'm not amateur in this business of love. Suppose I do some little monitoring... some serious learning about her... and see what I myself can find. Maybe you had a suspicious history of her when you were living, I can successfully cancel."

"Serves well, brother." This lady spirit's lips came back in a sneer. "But bear in mind that I didn't expect you to throw caution in the winds, as I dig her case this far. I expect you to desire to know how I actually dig them up; but it seems you choose to rather flirt with the danger."

Mr. Wyi Worri was shaking again. Real tremor down his legs. "Jesus knows, sis, I'm really afraid to even hear them. I might not like the effect."

"Be a man; it's better than not knowing," the lady phantom told him finally. "In sexual relationship... this kind paraded as true love... and maybe nooses believed to be put around each other's neck, as to be guided towards matrimonial end... I've got to think sceptical things that give lovers the willies. I sought and found things sly and scheming they wouldn't know about their partners. At least, my chilling eye-opener interpreted them deplorable, incorrigible, heartless or deceptive. One day I'd found out this one about MyAngel, my bosom home girl, though it'd been telling.

"It was real funny at first, then it wasn't so funny. I picked up suspicion on the change on her body and tried to level with her. You know what it had taken me? Some few prodding questions about her weight and complexion. She didn't admit herself pregnant, but she admitted some signs of added plumpness and paler complexion are quite signals of early pregnancy." The ghost looked at Mr. Wyi Worri and smiled. "See how amateur you can be in that angle of relationship. This was detected before she visited you around January, after some year gab you saw her last; do you understand?"

How could he understand this ugly raise of head of this pregnancy again—when what she wanted him to understand was rather making breathing hard again? "And if this was say before she visited after one year gab?"

The ghost held out her hand. "See what you can do in that angle." It watched him. "Or maybe I'm only making a delicate suspicion?"

"And if, against your nature, you are… even though you seem pretty cocky?"

"I can still come out to say it," it responded.

"Fine, you think I didn't try to find out who actually has the baby she's carrying?" …*But, hell, man, you went to the hospital when she encountered stomach upset and the doctor suggested she run a pregnancy test!* Yeah, but he tried her with that abortion suggestion and she vehemently refused that his adamant to the doctor's advice didn't count anymore. Or was she wiser than him, with that smart refusal? "Hell, sis, I tried."

The phantom nodded and looked around; the warning plain in her frail face. "If you'd tried and didn't dig up anything, brother, you were just stupidly nuts about MyAngel, my friend."

"Stupidly nuts! Before or after I made love to her and she told me she was pregnant later?'

"That depends on how amateur you were, or how cunny she was," she told him.

He felt around for words, and then he came out with it. "What am I going to do about it?"

"Find out first; what's the problem with you, brother? Try and remember! Calculate things! Was her attitude cocky or strange or this or that? How did you find her really within you, when she visited; were you observant? Maybe you were; what was your suspicion inside that you tried to know who has truly fathered the babe? How soon and ready she told you she was pregnant. Maybe you were reading her safe-period, was she really at the safe or wrong period going in line with the time she saw her pregnancy? By the virtue of your steady relationship, you've said hell to safe sex, what chances do you have for health and future now you sit there like a dumb asking what you're going to do about it?"

His face tightened with pain. "Why my girl... why her with all these vulgarities?"

"Because she played me a smart one when she denied my trusted suspicion, and still look forward to play you a fast one... perhaps as failsafe; do you understand now?"

"Goddamn it!" he hissed courageously. "Don't place everything on her! You're not sure, you know... even if you're a spirit."

"You're still nuts about her?"

"No," he glanced about again, his face wrinkling up. "No; if it's stupid, I'm not. But she's my fiancée, and maybe that makes the difference."

"How much do you still believe in her?"

"Much enough... and cool enough... and true enough... to know she wasn't a fake to that height, if at all she was."

"Brother," the she-spirit said; "I was a living woman, and I tell you this truth. In the years that I knew relationship about man and woman, I found out that no man knows a damn thing about a woman... and that goes double when he's in love with her. And now you're not just in naïve love, but stupidly nuts about MyAngel." She leaned over his face. "When you tried to find out things about her pregnancy, did you read her oestrus circle?"

He looked at the ghost. "It was so long she wasn't near, along the line I miscounted; but she told it anyway?"

"Right. Did you run a test and maybe know actual old that foetus was?"

"Why that height? Remember she's a darling and deserves some element of trust."

"Huh! But maybe it was this particular pregnancy I talked she shoved to you, and I keep saying, for a purpose other than using it to consolidate her position in your love."

He said; "Well, sis, thank you for the mare's nest." He stood and felt his balance jerky. It was high time she should disappear. "Having you around is an awful help, aw... you know what? I'll still take her as my wife no matter what she was."

"That's okay... though I'm still waiting for the upshot." She wasn't going to disappear yet. "The big story... and maybe more." The ghost grinned undauntedly.

"Yeah, you mean as long as she was a fake... like keeping me for a stopgap, or failsafe? But she's not anymore, sis!"

The lady phantom breathed a nasty curse. She was moving out instead. "A man, who doesn't know where rain started to beat him, can't know where he dried his body."

"There's something I forget to remind us," he said. "MyAngel and I were nuts about each other, and this led us to take vows of matrimony in the presence of God on our own. Now, do you think she's using me as a failsafe and stopgap? When she's still professing that love?"

"Just angles of possibilities. Nothing's new on earth to stupidly shrug out this obvious..." she stopped and swung to face him; "If you think spirits can frame things and I framed this, which I know you don't, I'll appear again to her face and say it, and then tell why I was a confederate for years and suddenly was fretting over the matter of you believing on her love. Now..." she nodded retrospectively; "you're a sucker for perfidious love, *Jesus*, brother, it's for your good, if you'll survive it easily yet."

He grabbed the wraith of his cousin before it could turn away again, and probably disappear; "Okay, sis; but I'm going to backtrack over your story, you know."

"I expect that."

"Then I promise you, for my good, I'll confront her."

"I expect that as well."

"And…" he started but Iris, the goddess from Morpheus, in the wraith of Chinonso, his cousin and MyAngel's bosom friend, finally missed there in his hands.

Could it be the doctor's hunch was right?

Later, Mr. Wyiwori was counting traumatically, *from ninth till now is seventy one days old; from thirteenth till now is sixty seven days old; and from sixteenth till now is sixty four days old.*

Chapter Seven

When Mr. Wyi Worri got to Miss Iyebiye's house, she had not come out. He greeted her elder sister, who was going out for her work with the little cousin, and went straight to her room—she was sleeping, curling up on her side. He wished he had right to lie there and let that touching sleeping face bury against his chest. He tucked a cover around her legs, and moved to the sitting room. The woman of the house had left, so the house was freer, and he felt like to serve himself a cup of tea. He had almost had the breakfast when he heard Miss Iyebiye come through the door. Her weavon hair looked like scattered in a wild heavy petting. He wished he had right for many things—yeah, to do many things.

"Good morning," she greeted; her smile that accompanied that was quite warm.

She was wearing a white quitted house-semi that didn't really conceal a thing—but that wasn't his problem now. "Nice morning." He grinned. "Sit down and join me. As you can see I'm tucking into a breakfast I served myself."

Miss Iyebiye first walked to a cushion and picked a cap which she tucked up her hair under it. "I wanted to come over to your house this morning and greet her, Mister Wyi Worri." She pulled out a chair with her toe and sat.

"She left back yesterday, girl. All the same, I'm in a situation that comes to a head. In the offing—an imminent harbinger."

Her eyes were curious. "Imminent harbinger?"

"Yeah; I'm putting on a red-alert on a rocky union that goes seriously ominous. Gawd, the prognosis is breaking my heart… my ingenuous heart."

Her eyebrows made two surprising arcs.

"I had a disturbing premonitory dream last night. That makes twice they came."

"They came and portend?"

"I wouldn't like to be a doomsayer of my own woe," he lamented; "but it so breaks my heart. This, *Omni*, is highly unforeseen!"

"Unforeseen…the presage…your prognostication… what?" She was just in the fog.

"I wish I'm a trustworthy psychic or seer here; have you noticed I was seeing her as the life I live?"

"Why, certainly! Her, is it not MyAngel, the lady who…"

"Who I'm in love with. My girlfriend I so showed you," he finished.

Miss Iyebiye frowned and nevertheless sipped her tea. "She's your fiancée too."

"Uh-huh. And now she's mysteriously complicated. I want to find out if these visionary foreboding eye-openers are anything reflection of what is happening about her in reality." He watched her. "How common is it for a young vibrant lady of twenty five to have some darn bleeding… I mean, for the reason of lack of pregnancy hormone?"

"Not very easy, but common, yes. It's been observed. Do you think the trait is in her family, and she'd have it?"

"To the second question… maybe. I heard something about indiscriminate abortions the basic cause of such ill-fated problem on young ladies; do you know anything about it?" He eyed her probingly. "Of course, you have head for it by your profession."

"The case in pregnancies, especially of young ladies, may not be the basic causes; but it's possible, and it seems logical." She watched him doubtfully. "But why would she want to indulge in rampart abortions? At least any promising man would be glad and blessed to take her as his wife any time any day, if such unplanned member comes up?"

"That my fiancée…" *the goddamn mystery…* "is playing me up. She's…" he stopped in the middle of the sentence; "Girl, how good are you with trustworthiness—I mean, a hell of confidant?"

The tea cup was dropped, producing a tension clink against the tray. She read his vengeful expression and stiffened. "That's not nice to a fiancée."

"I don't do nice things when I'm unfairly treated, and on edge for it, Chrisette; but I want you to know. I should shut up my mouth because you and MyAngel are on somewhat rivalry, but if you sound off to anyone in scurrilous or defamatory gossip, you'll never be able to have my regard again. You understand that; don't you?"

She greased her face with hot indignation. "You don't have to tell me anything!" she snapped.

"No, I don't have to; but I can hold myself a bit reasonably when I think someone out here cares to share my troubles. Listen, sieve and perm all you want to, but keep it to yourself. Like I was saying about MyAngel, my fiancée, she's double-booking and carrying a baby I suspected I have no true business. She has it all arranged so in case she's unable to get rid of it, she'd be able to shove everything on me. Well, that may just be what is happening. She's the one pulling the divine love, she's still the one doing the desecration, and I'm taking the dopey fools-paradise for it."

"You… you…" Miss Iyebiye's eyes dilated; she was not just getting it. She adjusted all herself over the chair. A position that allowed her sit with her legs tucking up under her. "You went to the hospital with her?"

"Yeah, and saw a doctor. He was going to diagnose her for an ailment that struck her chest and down the stomach the second night the first time she visited me earlier this year, but found out she might be pregnant and advised us to go for a test…

pregnancy test." He watched her. "True, but we didn't go for that test, and nobody bordered until now; how could we border, after all!"

"You're sure about this?" she still asked.

"As sure as I can be, during my damning time, without any proof. If I know more about how doctors know a pregnancy, just a day old pregnancy, without carrying out any medical test, I'd have put that question in the right place."

Her eyebrows went up again—and even higher this time. "But you... you've been having..."

"I never made love to her in ages before she came," he said; "because of prudish distance in our residing stations. You're the first person I've told this, and you're going to be the last. For the two years I've known her, and a year now we had our engagement, it was only on two occasions we had so celebrated our consummation of love. The period we celebrated our oath of betrothal, and the period she visited. I'm just a guy who has a torrid fiancée that hops about with careless sexual escapades, at the expense of his sex-starved sacrificial love."

Anyway, Mr. Wyi Worri gave her the dreams with few citation of probing aphorisms, and she just sat there with her mouth open trying to absorb them all. And if not he motioned her to eat while she was listening, she wouldn't have even finished about the same time he did with his story.

"It's just incredible, really. Nobody would think differently!" she said at last.

"Not so now the futurist visions have portended. I'm going to play the game right up to the hilt until I find out why this visionary fact had hunted me in the dreams, and now the baby is refusing to stay there in the womb for some obscure shortage of progesterone." He grinned bitterly. "And sometimes I think she was trying to explain, in addition, there was problem of wrong positional location of the foetus. You're wondering why I bother telling you all this; it's because I'm going to need you."

"What do you want me to do?"

"I want you to help me do a research, or as you've known already, write out things for me... things about oestrus circle, you know, safe period. Foetus formation. Hormonal changes and imbalance. And the rest of them. Nurses are good at teaching things like that, right? Try and write out any other cause in your discipline other than incessant abortions or maybe in line with trait of a family or maybe advancement in maternal age."

"Well, aside occurring from either of them, you have other causes like uterus abnormalities. You still have some causes like tract infection or tissue rejection… and don't forget, chromosomal problems due to a parent's genes are, however, a big possibility."

"That's all right. Her case may be traced to indiscriminate abortions; because if her mother, who I know, had continued to have baby at later advanced age, with no qualms and no hormone replacement therapy, she's probably not going to have it in her trait as problem at twenty five. After all, genetic problems occur with older parents. She could be cooking up a story like that to go with miscarriage, while she actually gets rid of the controversial baby herself… and no one can start asking questions." He watched her and grinned bitterly again. "You see, I know… yeah, I know… I'm living in quite awful fools-paradise, but not unwittingly. Yeah, I know, not slavishly."

She pushed her cup back; Mr. Wyi Worri watched that and got up rather.

"Alright, Mister Wyi Worri, you can count on my confidentiality if you want to. I'll use this morning and write out those things in a way an average man would understand them. I'll bring them to you."

"Yeah, I count on you. And I won't wait up for it." He grinned.

"Then, you'll be back a little time."

Tentatively, he watched her up and down. "What else, perhaps?"

"Kiss?" She tilted her head up and half closed her eyes—ready.

"Uh-uh, I won't think you didn't scrub before eating."

"Stupid boy," she hit him—still ready.

"You beat me, honey… because I still won't mind you didn't

wash before coming to sit here with me?"

"You're a hopeless fellow, I tell you." She backed off.

"*Ugh*, I wouldn't know."

She pursed with disabuseness.

Miss Iyebiye was in truth a pretty dish. All right. A little on the lovelorn side when you came close, and you didn't take away the pity that lurked in the corner around her failed ransacked love. She was a million the dough under nobles oblige, and two million in therapeutic melting partnership. And would have to be a dime a dozen as the so much needed inamorata. Though.

"I wouldn't—God knows why," he confessed and walked out.

Chapter*Eight*

Mr. Wyi Worri prowled about his room with heavy sense of frustration. She wouldn't pick his calls of three stubborn but concerned days now. No, she wouldn't dare! She would as well take a gun and put it to his head and blast it, sending his brain scattered in the mid-air—at least, sending him to Elysian field at last.

It was five months gone her pregnancy, and roughly two months she last visited. But then it was roughly a month come by he would satisfactorily complete his one year national service. He was a 2008 batch B, and the second batch out of the three consistent batches in a year. Next month July was the pupated completion cycle, and all the members of this batch B was holding a Pre-Passing Out party this Friday night—and all the male folks at least were expected to flow in as *doubles*. And he, Mr. Wyi Worri, was the most celebrated envious double in his union with MyAngel.

But she had desperately loved him, he thought as he paced about the more. It was *doggon* this blooming incapacity of her living above inconstancy! This kittenish tendency that invariably belied the apparent integrity of her vow!

He brought his hand a thousand times up again to his ear. The phone was ringing normally, but then it was cancelled, and it beeped a *user busy* tone. He tried it again and again and again and lastly again. It was, of course, all not available. She had put off her phone device again today.

He nodded spitefully and shrugged and decided to leave her alone. He checked his handset for time; it was late already by eight.

Damned, she was a flirt! They would have thought better before climbing to that altar.

The party had just ended a little over 3am, and they were all scattered in *twos* about the compound, laughing and chatting salaciously. And this two were sitting in a table quite separate, taking the last of their drinks.

Mr. Wyi Worri picked up his bottle again, wondering if they finished their drinks now and leave, he would be lonesome; "This can only keep me dangerously tipsy," he said dolefully.

"Marry the fantasy," Miss Iyebiye said. "Who knows, she may have arrived as we left; and she'll never let this leering mode go by... for sure."

"I guess it's got to a breaking point." He threw the empty can under the table, and shoved the plate of his remaining meat away to Miss Iyebiye. "I think I'm in the midst of psychotic break right now."

Miss Iyebiye watched the overburdened Mr. Wyi Worri with some deep pathetic feeling. "So tell me exactly what's happening now between you and your fiancée."

"I sensed the bitch cheating and still playing me expensively. Nothing much more to tell than that."

"But she wouldn't just disgrace and trash such big feeling you have for her, without being a bit penitent?"

"Hell, no! She just felt it was deplorably inadvisable to lose my trust that scurrilous way... and she lunged into another woeful tangent and showed me how she could disdainfully disappoint me again." He cleaned his mouth with his handkerchief. His eyes were sober and lugubrious. "It did happen we arranged to attend this party together, and she should come over a day before, but she didn't and wouldn't pick my hell of calls. I wanted to know if there was any trouble, and when my paging became intolerable she simply put off her set. You know I had those prognostic dreams..." he stopped; frustration was choking him to cry.

"Now, what's wrong with you, Mister Wyi Worri?" she said, leering at the pity scenario. "Do you have a death wish just for mere disappointment, or something? I thought that you're worldly and blasé... that you're actually on great terms with fun-loving atmosphere like we just had? That you should know it's really unnecessary, and a little stupid, to become neurotic about mere superstitions... however prophetic? That you should think a worldly lady of our time can always do some wrong in love business? Grass doesn't grow on a busy road; don't you know she wouldn't back up love infallibly with this distance? There must be a point when the passionate love yearns for some douse in the dry boring abstinence, and an alternative of doing it with a third party gives a new level of satisfaction."

Mr. Wyi Worri toyed a moment with the possibility of that truthful incidence of his fiancée' treacherous glitches. "You know, MyAngel was a good lady; she believed in me... my clingy love... my helpless unadulterated love... our envious love... our undiluted love..." he watched Miss Iyebiye vulnerably; "Now, tell me; is there any sincere way to take the easy way out other than this lousy way I feel about it? It's love we're talking about here! And it's not out of place if I'm helplessly buried in it, as the horrible dirt flies. That's the theory, sweetheart. The theory of this love I'm thinking about here. I actually thought she felt bad about the whole thing... about giving me the chance to suspect her love; but what happened? At the end of the day I was only a joker. A dreamer. She broke my heart flagrantly again. When all is said and done, woe bestride me, she'd probably come to me knowing full well I wouldn't survive a jot without her love... her shoddy love... and she'd come to me this with every colossal nerve and right of love..."he blew his almost dry nose, anyway; "yeah, right of love."

Miss Iyebiye took his hand. She remembered the remaining meat shifted to her, and picked it and threw it into her mouth. "I don't know again how to help fondly in this pitiful circumstance, Mister Wyi Worri. It's rather dangerous involving in some touching troilism, and then have to rely on some inimitable asceticism to actually survive?"

"I just want to feel like a babe in your arms, Miss Iyebiye. I just want you to hold me and put me to bed, and lull me to sleep in a little while. You don't have to snog, and you don't have to be like come-hither succour, or you fall into a sick help that rather haunts."

Miss Iyebiye stared into the space, digesting his suggestion.

"What do you say?" He continued, sliding out of his chair.

"I'll follow you to your house and sooth you to sleep, don't worry." She was obliging nevertheless.

But back here on his bed, the fact that he was so close to this love that actually was eluded him where he had right for it, froze him out finally—And he found himself vengefully pressing the buttons of his handset for this message:-

My Angel, I still wonder why you take me as a fool despite my experience with ladies. You should have known I would know when a lady is fake. I wanted to love you, true, but it doesn't mean I'm desperate to marry you with mysterious questionable characters.

You weren't picking my calls, but I can still reach you by this. I know you don't have any true story to cover up your perfidy yesterday—then I wish to tell you that you're not straight forward, and my love is simply too ingenuous for your kind.

It's not just your unfaithfulness, but your trickiness, lies, pride, unconcern, disrespect, mystery and incorrigibility—and they are clearly not what I want.

You claimed I'm the father of that baby you're carrying, but with this life you're living, I will never ever trust that but with reasonable confirmation—Until it is born.

From my life, My Angel, goodbye and good radiance.

Chapter*Nine*

*L*ying there on his bed with his stomach, Mr. Wyi Worri booted his laptop, inserted his modem and waited. Then he checked his inbox for a message.

Re; There is.

Unfortunately we are unable to come to an alternative arrangement regarding the payment conditions of your publication.

'In The World of Eve' is a quite extraordinary very ambitious work of considerable scope and great fascination. And in the case of this book, the payment to cover the publication would be £4,800. This would usually be paid in four equal instalments as follows;-

£1,200 on signing the contract.

£1,200 on your approval of the edited manuscript.

£1,200 on your approval of the page proofs.

£1,200 on printing.

The book would be presented flat bound, with a reinforced gloss paperback cover and a full colour cover design. The total publication process takes approximately six months from signing the contract to receiving your complimentary Author's advance copies.

We believe this book could also find a readership in the USA, so we would publish both in USA and the UK if we proceed.

Incidentally, if you pay the whole amount in one payment at the beginning, you can deduct 10% from the total.

If our programme meets with your approval please let us know, and we will be pleased to prepare and send you a contract for the publication of the book.

Yours sincerely,
Dave Moriho
Group Publication Director.
Athena Press Limited.

Jesus Christ, could success be so close, like this, and still far!

£4,800! Approximately one point three million naira in his country's currency! How could their programme meet with his approval when his mother, the breadwinner, was not receiving anything beyond seventy thousand naira as monthly salary? Now the whole top-rated recommendation and acceptance of his book as publishable by this topflight publisher, situated at the Great Britain, had become a mere blind alley!

When Mr. Wyi Worri received their publication system, he had belief his works merited publication and would be pleased to work with them on publishing at least one of his books. He had believed the quantum leap was a ticket of rip-roaring break through, and then he had thought if his book had a rosy potential, a help, which they would gain afterwards, could come—and he had written to them based on that with the subject, *'There is'*.

But there is. Yeah, there was really a way out. A cherry compromise synonymous to dues-ex-machine. A benefit of an agent of Dominus Vobiscum Investments Ltd, a financial institution he was a staff, that was equivalent to dues-ex-machine. He was sure because it was enshrined there on page 8 of the abridged profile of this institution he was a bona-fide agent.

Next Mr. Wyi Worri wrote;-

Wyi Worri,
Ezimagu Nunya Isuikwuato,
Abia State.
03/07/2009

The CEO,
Dominus Vobiscum Investment Ltd,
Enugu.
Enugu State.
Sir,

AN APPLICATION FOR FINANCIAL ASSISTANCE.

I'm humbly applying for a loan of one million two hundred thousand naira to enable me finance the publication of a book of international recognition.

My name is Wyi Worri, a representative of the firm at Owerri branch. I have a book that have been sanctioned okay for publication by the editorial department of Athena Press Limited, London, Queen's House, 2 holly Road, Twickenhan, TW1 4GE9 (with registered No. 4308545, and registered office, 1 South Street Chichester, West Sussex, P109 IEH). After going through the book they placed the cost at 4,800 pounds.

I shall refund the loan immediately I have the launching and receiving of royalties of the book. I promise to abide to any agreement I shall have with the firm.

Thanks in anticipation.

Yours faithfully,
Wyi Worri.

Chapter *Ten*

Mr. Wyi Worri saw Miss Iyebiye come to his door, walk into the room and put down the bag she was carrying. It was a drama, but he watched that and shrugged when she left again. Two minutes later she came back and wasn't alone. MyAngel was with her. The arrant lover looked bubbly. Real bubbly. He called her a bitch as he lashed out, sending his fist landing against the reading table with the rude curse. The two ladies leered at him and stayed out of range. All he did was make his frustration put the squeeze on him the more.

"You know why this action here is purely ungentlemanly; don't you, Mister Wyi Worri?" Miss Iyebiye wondered of him.

"But she knows she's not welcomed here; I warned her. She thinks she's pretty smart!" he muttered hotly.

"Yes, I know," MyAngel agreed, drawing the bag Miss Iyebiye dropped at the middle of the room near the door, leaned on this door and waited for him to act another thing.

The ladies would have still been waiting standing there like that, if Prince Williams didn't walk in. They looked at him, and Miss Iyebiye was kind of see if MyAngel would get tossed out or not.

But Prince Williams said; "See, Mister Wyi Worri, for a

healthy relationship, it's good to give a measure of space to each other; becoming too possessive of partner's time or attention can surely smother a relationship." He handed a phone message to Mr. Wyi Worri and added tonelessly; "It's an apology from her; very contrite and all that. MyAngel, your fiancée, is free based on inconveniences beyond her control; so you'll put away your punishment and lift your ban."

The message said;-

Please help me tell him, I truly apologize. I would have made it for the party, but it was just beyond me. The days, my heart was down and my head spinning around from the nefarious weight of all his mistrust. He always insists on getting his way and in doing this, constantly makes me feel guilty, stupid and worthless. Abusively, he checks up on my where about, makes threat and gives ultimatums unnecessarily. Accusing me of flirting indecently with men when there is no basis for doing so—And now it's unfortunate, under these pressures, all I suffered, I finally miscarried.

I finally miscarried, instant red came into Mr. Wyi Worri's face, but he fought to control how mad he was by the way he spoke. "It beats my imagination you were mixed up with her, Prince Williams." His voice was calm—just like cold. "I didn't want to think so because you used to be a nice pal... like a brother."

"So you were, Mister Wyi Worri." Prince Williams had ice of his own.

Mr. Wyi Worri's face turned and pointed at MyAngel. "Now you've got friends, MyAngel?Now you've got friends who can pull strings and pull a rabbit out of a hat for you this way, because somebody is afraid of getting in wrong with my genuine love for you? Some other person even went the trouble of putting up your accomplice; so you have some very powerful friends all of a surprise?" His eyes shifted to Miss Iyebiye and Prince Williams a moment, before coming back to MyAngel. "You're going to need them, lady, but they'll never be able to help you enough." He looked at Miss Iyebiye; "Yeah, if you truly want to help."

"The common good takes priority over the individual good here, Mr. Wyi Worri." Prince Williams said.

Mr. Wyi Worri's face didn't hide any of his anger. "I'm the one that bears the brunt here, Prince Williams; what do you mean by *common good*?"

"Popular opinion, Mister Wyi Worri."

"That when it's unjust it should be obeyed?" Mr. Wyi Worri flared. "Tell me, Prince Williams!"

"Mister Wyi Worri, I'll like to define you the common good here as the *sum total of individual good which in no way stands against the individual good*," Prince Williams said seriously. "In such case, the individual good can never be justified in refusing to obey the laws of common good."

Mr. Wyi Worri watched Prince Williams truculently. He knew he was an ex-seminarian—a product of Plato, or maybe a direct offspring of Socrates. He knew he was a philosopher and a good one too. Maybe a beta plus. But he also knew he was injuriously wrong in this, and he snapped vociferously; "Even that eccentric Socrates you borrowed his incongruent idea here still on one side, believed that individual good has right to contradict and be against common good! Give me a space here; I have the right of caveat emptor."

"Don't be a larrikin, Mister Wyi Worri," Miss Iyebiye chided.

"Yes… no man, however wise, can win judgment against his clan." Prince Williams expensively came again, with that adage.

"Gawd, praxis certainly don't pull my punches!" Mr. Wyi Worri flared the more. "You know what? You were only part of this clan because my big-heart wished; trust me, what you're now are simply messengers. And a messenger is not supposed to be a judge, and God knows, does not choose the massage he'll carry."

"Mister Wyi Worri, the cost of peace is high, but it's worth the price," Miss Iyebiye said and signalled MyAngel to go and sit, and then edged out of the room, closing the door.

MyAngel managed to shuffle across to the bed after a second signal to go and sit from Prince Williams. She perched on the edge of the bed.

Mr. Wyi Worri watched that and took some steps close to Prince Williams—his disappointment oozing out of every pore. "Don't ever call me your brother, Prince Williams. Never again;

do you understand?" He swung on his heels and reached for the doorknob.

"Mister Wyi Worri," Prince Williams said.

Mr. Wyi Worri barely looked back.

"We used to be best of friends... close pals," Prince Williams said again.

"I'm afraid, no more."

"You used to be an understanding lover, too," MyAngel put in.

Mr. Wyi Worri looked all the way back, his hand still on the door. "No more."

"When you finally realize that it's possible for even a worldly brain like yours to be wrong and paranoid, maybe you'll fancy my brotherly tough love to sustain the bonds of this union. You're not smarter than me in love business, and I say, MyAngel, your fiancée, never was that player. Think about it sometime."

Mr. Wyi Worri thought about it. For at least two seconds. Then he opened the door and slammed it behind him so hard that if it wasn't his own door, one would think he wanted it come of the hinges.

What a sell-out—an unthinkable sell-out! He cursed and cursed. He remembered every curse word he had learnt and strung them out in a row, as he trotted out blind with rage— edging towards any palliative honky-tonk spot his wandering movement might take him to.

The whole pointing precognition was a screwed-up mess— yeah, if ever he saw one. Everybody wanted him wrong, but she was the wrong. Miss Iyebiye wanted him wrong. Prince Williams wanted him wrong. Even a confidant and a correct pal, *Gawd!*

But Miss Iyebiye had understood his plight, believed it and even sympathized with him. And Prince Williams had stood behind him in the race... but now it started going grubby and shoddy against him, he was prepared to chastise him instead.

Damned! Damned!

*E*vidently, there was some communication between the people on the streets and these upsetting visitors. The door was opened as Mr. Wyi Worri was doing justice to some bottles of drink around his table, and a courtesy waiter on a striped uniform grinned and ushered himself in. He closed the door as if he knew Mr. Wyi Worri was in this solitary section because he didn't really want a company, and said; "Sir, some ladies want to see you; but you can cancel it."

Anyway Mr. Wyi Worri was rather lonesome and didn't even have time to do that. Miss Iyebiye and MyAngel had found his door and come in before he could weigh considerations, nodded greetings and pulled chairs up for themselves.

Mr. Wyi Worri said earlier the errant fiancée was bubbly, yeah, as effervescent as the lady of page girl. Strictly vivacious in a decisive bib and tucke suit, looking like she stepped out of the pages of a magazine. Her hair was freshly braided and arranged in a splashy coiffure, and for a second he wished it was some love cuddle he was giving her draw, instead of being here with foreboding jealousy, for a clairvoyance dangerously unheeded, and vicious pain at heart to keep it intolerable.

Mr. Wyi Worri allowed them sit down, and even cross their legs, before he shuddered abominably, to show he was still teed off about something.

"Surely you have something extra on your mind, Mister Wyi Worri?" Miss Iyebiye said.

"That's a mild way of putting it. Gawd, the way she seems to move events around to suit her exoneration, is quite disturbing!"

"Like this afternoon," MyAngel joshed in and even smiled.

"Like moments ago; do you realize that henpecked leverage?" He demanded of Miss Iyebiye, ignoring MyAngel. "She did, you see; but do you?"

"Sort of…" Miss Iyebiye said, and looking at MyAngel, she continued instead; "Perhaps you better explain, in case I miss a point. Tell him; you suffered these troubles, so you're more familiar with the situation than I am."

"He won't listen to me, tell him anyhow," MyAngel said.

"Okay," Miss Iyebiye pressed her fingers. "We're after two things; I'll start it that way. A case of deception in a conjugal world of oaths and devotion, and a couple of double-dating against the modus operandi of a world of fidelity. Your disregard has spread this case wide open as far as Mister Wyi Worri, your fiancé, here, is concerned. Until this afternoon you visited and Prince Williams brought your vindication, you were tagged for both abominable aberrations; now there's a reason to believe that you never pulled anything for the heck of it.

"Let's look at it this way; MyAngel, as a true lover, wasn't concerned with imposture and inconstancy… it was clingy and sacrificial love that she was after. She was doing fine until this love happened to get her into sudden implication of lovemaking with reckless motherhood, then all her good works eroded away when the pregnancy suddenly started giving trouble, and finally washed out by some long stubborn bleeding… giving her fiancé foreboding mind that formed suspicious prognosis in disturbing dreams. These prognostications are supposed to have happened, or been happening, with this *misread* disappointment caused by some inconveniences beyond her control."

"Unfairly misread," MyAngel ventured another joshed remark.

"Shut up!" Mr. Wyi Worri scorned readily.

"However," Miss Iyebiye continued; "After she dodged from picking his calls, it made the case certain, and in one respect, the heat was directed away from the value of sacrifice she put there to keep his baby.

"Now we know this much, Mister Wyi Worri probably has the wrong notion…even as the actual divination of those strange dreams hasn't been known yet. We know that after she had that conception, Mister Wyi Worri, her fiancé, put so much brazen mistrust over the actual father of her baby. And again, she and the unborn child were pretty in disagreement, until it finally got aborted spontaneously… perhaps. But the question there to Mr. Wyi Worri, her fiancé, was spontaneously or induced, at the end of the day, the reality was that the baby wouldn't be source of verification.

"Now for the reason of uncertain cause of this gruesome termination, it's possible she'd taken abortion induced drugs to get rid of it, as long as it affords her some let-out or alibi… and there's no doubt his inkling would shrink out… and she could have enough guilty trip to give him, since in the first place she showed huge sacrificial love when she refused to get rid of it. Perhaps the baby was stubborn and refused to be washed out, and she began to suffer tortures of long bleeding, and now he has enough guilty conscience to make the life-in-danger sacrifice scourge him unfairly. But remember this; it was still a big suspicion… and if she could get away without his vindictive alarm button smashing her, a couple of vengeful moves, perhaps actually two-timing him, could make for some pretty revenge. She might have very well taken that questionable venture of the eventful day… without minding her grandiose vow… and made some sexual day-out with some rival."

MyAngel gave a curt laugh. "Or she might have very well made another vow of betrothal, and damned her previous with him."

Mr. Wyi Worri shook disapprovingly. "No, I like it the first way," he said; it could be dangerously sinister to imagine himself losing her, after all. He still loved her.

"Why?" MyAngel talked again, cutting his nostalgia.

But he wouldn't answer that.

"Because Mister Wyi Worri is still in love with her, that's why." It was Miss Iyebiye who said this. "Along the line, he got disappointed, forlorn, lovelorn, but never hopeless. The love he has for her is still great that he wouldn't love to appreciate her replacement." She threw a glance at Mr. Wyi Worri "Even at these disreputable incidents he associates her with." She added cattily.

"How did you get that?" MyAngel said, a little suspicious.

"I talked with him." Miss Iyebiye smiled. "Mister Wyi Worri, your fiancé, is a nice man; if I see him moody, I try to help him ease the load." She threw Mr. Wyi Worri another glance. "You mentioned something about damning your previous vow of conjugal bonding; I think that vow it's quite height of love," she said to MyAngel. "It's quite commendable."

Mr. Wyi Worri looked at Miss Iyebiye squarely. "*Doggon it*, her questionable ways have managed to cheapen them."

"No, your nefarious accusations have managed to cheapen them!" MyAngel flared. "And you know they're unsubstantiated!"

"But she can agree with me they're circumstantial!" Mr. Wyi Worri retorted back. "The nefarious accusations have managed rightly to cheapen the milky-mouse love; there's no need going into the polemical detail of how and particularly why they did it, but they found that she had a dubious kind of sudden trip into motherhood and bury and bury forever, the means that would have used to unravel the mystery."

"So?" MyAngel demanded heavily.

"So there's still the case of infidelity to be accounted for," he supplied darkly. "By the time you deliver, I'd have known the truth and you know. Yeah, after your conception on January ninth or thirteenth or sixteenth, no alibi would breathe a second alive, if you put to bed a full blown baby a month or two before nine months, by my own calculation."

Miss Iyebiye saw the frown on MyAngel's face. "The point is this, Mister Wyi Worri, you're not trying to make this case a private one any longer. And since it's gone free-wheeling, the code of conjugal conduct has its own inalienable rule officially assign to it, and applicable in conjunction with discipline. Now, Mister Wyi Worri, you're sort of at the centre of the unguarded disputation; you can bust-up things if you're not careful."

Mr. Wyi Worri stood up and watched Miss Iyebiye in a new wary fashion. "In other words, I'll have to pull in my horns?"

"The matrimonial journey you've blissfully started, the divine destination and favour, is what matters. I know you still love her…" Miss Iyebiye turned to MyAngel; "And you too."

MyAngel wouldn't know whether that sentence was to be answered or not, but she could feel Mr. Wyi Worri's eyes on her, and she waited to see what he would say.

Mr. Wyi Worri said; "Code of conjugal conduct, what is it there for?"

A moment pause and Miss Iyebiye said; "Primarily complement, then trust and respect."

"That's very good," he told her; "very good. My love, it wants complement too. But that doesn't come it all. Me, myself, I, want a whole hell of people, who care to know, that Mister Wyi Worri was restive because he didn't have and couldn't have and wouldn't have anything to do with inconstant love of deceit, infidelity and disregard. I want to prove that there's still a decent chaste thing to be proud of in a young man that even women with all their uppity protective pride, couldn't keep as it's called for in a conjugal union... because of their seamy liberated hot panties. And you know how I'm going to do it?"

The two ladies were waiting for him to say them, and he didn't—he said; "No, I won't get the horns pulled in; do you understand that, Chrisette? They don't get pulled in... not a bit. My bald-faced disputation could bust-up things some, but there's more a chance that some brother elsewhere would bust it up shamefully for me first." He waited, expecting an argument, but didn't get any.

Now Miss Iyebiye hit her head in confusing fashion. "I know if you don't prevent a crack, you'll build a new wall. I understand quite well how you feel, Mister Wyi Worri, but please understand this; I'm not trying to interfere with your... um... crusade. I know the kind of issue you're dealing with, and I don't want it to be in further inconvenient scandals before you come to the divination of those dreams. You know, nevertheless, dreams sometimes come in reality pure opposite."

"Further inconvenient scandals? Do mean the type I could get if my style forces her to finally give me the kiss off? The old heave-ho?"

"Yes, the remaining teeth should chew with caution until the aching tooth is removed; you're walking blind folded through the dangerous neighbourhood, and it's like one who digs a cricket hole with a pestle and ends up blocking the hole."

Mr. Wyi Worri looked at MyAngel. "Madam, do you feel the prosaic way too?"

"More or less," MyAngel even confided. "With all intends and purposes, you're sullying my huge love to scandalous farce. I'm a lady that needs some trust and respect to keep my rare love. Look at you, my fiancé, you're screwing up the trust and respect pretty nicely."

"Yes… pretty nicely," Miss Iyebiye said.

"Then cui bono?"

"Cui bono?" Miss Iyebiye didn't understand.

"If MyAngel is to be discharged and acquitted, and she actually pulled the treacherous stunt, which the divination must come unbearably, are you willing to console me? Chrisette, are you willing to redress the balance?"

Miss Iyebiye stood and got mad first, then dropped her eyes. "This is a case of love-relationship, cheating on love, Mister Wyi Worri, I can't be in position to redress the balance."

"Fuck…" Mr. Wyi Worri said and was going to say more, when the words there in his mouth couldn't come out again. His mind was going around in a cute wary circle, making depth here and there… and the same home-truth started to appear, which was tendentious in a way, but with definite credence that painted a real picture of a cheat—a provoking cheat, because he couldn't go to redress a betrayal on love,by the modus Vivendi, the way it was equal and fair situation.

So instead of all the words he had stored up, he sat down back and said; "Any chance of getting some assurance of penitence and reparation?" He knew it from the atmosphere. He felt it strongly at each added moment of certain candour. Believe it—believe everything. As MyAngel was avoiding those calls, he knew a sizzling of some love escapade was taking place. She didn't have to claim wrongfully beleaguered, because just as she knew what she did, he knew what she did. Both of them knew what she had all about gone. And he had come to believe it just as he had come to believe the history of Second World War, that Adolf Hitler was guilty of the Jewish holocaust. Now he watched his girl. "MyAngel, I charged you by the innocent love I have for you, look unto God and say I was evil for accusing you. If you don't know, the way you boycotted our earlier arrangement, without informing me, only pushed me to rethink the mysteries around your pregnancy." He watched her some more, she wasn't ready to say anything, and he continued; "Well, I need insurance here. God knows…" he looked back at Miss Iyebiye; "I need some provisos here."

MyAngel stood out from her chair, watched Miss Iyebiye momentarily, and like she got a sleight of hand move on support, moved to Mr. Wyi Worri. Now she went on her hunkers, took his hand, and then looked up at his face; "Far beyond the call of love, as long as your love is there to lead me, I won't lose my way." She watched him and he wasn't yet ready to react. "You're forever in my heart, always in my mind, for there's no one I could love more than you." Now she was repeating words of her engagement vow. "All my love is for you because you're my true love, and I love you with all my heart." It seemed he reacted a little, but then nothing happened on that face of his. "My love for you is like an ocean, it goes down so deep. My love for you is like a rose, whose beauty you want to keep. I love you, sweetheart, for real." She concluded the pricey words.

But this was too melodramatic. Too propitiatory that Mr. Wyi Worri couldn't hold back some virtuous soft spot anymore. He watched MyAngel's face, everything he had accused her was expectantly hidden. Façade. Aye. When he thought them over again, he nodded. "Okay," he told them; "I'll pull in my horns." He, yeah, then took her unto himself.

Mr. Wyi Worri saw Prince Williams personally come looking for him. The bike he chartered came up their way, and he climbed down, waving off the ladies silently, and Mr. Wyi Worri watched them without much ado sashay across the road and flap down a taxi and climb in. The poor honest broker looked pretty upset and God knows, it didn't help his face any. He waved Mr. Wyi Worri to climb the bike, and he too without much ado climbed the bike. Prince Williams climbed behind him, and the rider made a U-turn and picked the way back into the hostelry, where Prince Williams quickly settled him and settled for a discussion.

"*Holy Mary*, you're acting on an impudent egoistic impulse, without being alert to the dangers!"

"Getting my head screwed right in love business. Thinking, you know, about it sometime."

"How?"

"Somehow you couldn't approve, chum."

"Another faux pas… man, another depredation?"

"Maybe, no."

"Nope? And that'll probably keep the relationship out of trouble more than anything else you can think of?"

"Yeah… it will," Mr. Wyi Worri made a concession.

"As long as you don't marry one anymore," Prince Williams sounded damned sour. He stood up, marched towards going away, but halted and waited until he had made sure Mr. Wyi Worri wasn't staying back and maybe demanding for drinks, then waved him over. "If you want some form of escapism for any solace, it'll be at the house of God. I hope you don't want me to believe that oath you took there in the presence of God, means little to you?" He watched his level of deviance; "You were impersonal, taking that arrogant leave because you were going to get stinking solace on alcohol… and you…"

"Yeah… and I was going to do it alone and without having your Band-Aid leverage in my hair; do you understand?" Mr. Wyi Worri sassily interrupted.

"Shut up and listen, if you try to win the love of a woman by holding a stick in one hand, you'll remain a bachelor for life," Prince Williams cautioned. "And now, listen and listen good; keeping relationship is not always a bed of roses, so you must try to correct each other's fault gently. Know that you can never find a perfect partner, but to involve the imperfect person perfectly. And lastly, the basis of every relationship is prayer. Make God, who you made me believe it was in His holy presence you made those vows, the foundation and bedrock of your relationship."

"Okay, okay, chum," Mr. Wyi Worri propitiated

Chapter *Eleven*

*H*e had gone to bed, a week after, when his handset buzzed around 11pm. He rolled over and reached out to the table to pick the disturbing device.

(Mister Wyi?)

"Speaking. Who's this?" He questioned the voice of a soft spoken woman over the phone.

(Do you really know about the love women give?)

Mr. Wyi Worri was instantly alert. "In what regard?"

(Something has happened where you believe this love.)

"Sis, can you be more specific?"

(You see, I can't say more… really.) Her distress was clear. (You need to find out what's going on out there about her!)

"Her? Which her?"

(Where you place your love; find out!)

The caller cut the line. It happened so fast. Mr. Wyi Worri brought the set on his face and stared at it, before he dropped it back. On a second thought he picked it again and dialled the number.

When a male voice this time answered he said brusquely; "This is Mister Wyi Worri, a corps member serving in Ondo state. I want this person that just called this line back on line.

Want me to wait?"

(Just a minute, please.)

He waited.

(She's just disappeared; well, this end is a phone booth on the streets of Lagos... around Sele.)

Streets of Lagos! "Okay, thanks."

You need to find out! Find out what? His brain troubled. Yeah what? *What's going on about her!* But about who? Yeah, *'who'* was the question. Though it seemed there was no answer to it there, but a snapshot to answer it was there. *Where you place your love! 'You'*, him now! Place his love!

MyAngel was living in Lagos, where she was studying catering after leaving her job as a receptionist—*MyAngel again!* No, too raw. Aye, raw all the way round. Raw in regard to the information. Raw in the sense a raw deal. He cursed the troubling faculty and tried to switch it off the ricocheted thoughts that led to last time woeful accusations. It was unfounded and he had tried to repress any retread retracting.

He fought himself mentally. He wished this wasn't like a case of his last two rites of passage. The period even his youthful delinquency could not help reducing the woe-be-gone worry he whined with fixatedly. This particular delinquency was his life he had surprisingly found gone completely in oblivion. The one time dared rite of passage. The aspect of his feral demeanour he had been forgotten—too mindless to mention all along his records.

It was during the time of his sophomore, between his second and third year in higher institution. And it all started when he found ordinarily it was intractable to realize one of his core age-long dreams about his anatomy. When it was obvious that, by virtue of nature, sizeable flesh upon his bones had really eluded him—placing him below appreciating any good appetite for food. When all the multi-vitamin drugs and orthodox appetizers found themselves incapacitated to solve his problem. Aye, incapacitated because it was raw nature they were combating with.

'Guy, dope is your solution', they had told him, and he made

instantaneous caring friends and felt belonging—Fake sense of caring and belonging, anyway. They were always obliging, along, and benevolently making the illegal stuff handy for his consumption. His conscience was blurred. In fact, he successfully sold it out for some aspects of undisciplined human chemistry of high level immorality. A world he wrong-headedly thought the inordinate urge was a trait—not finest trait, anyway—and it had followed familially, and willy-nilly he believed, incorrigibly. And he had thought unless he fought it out with some daredevil undertaking, and with so much temerity and contempt.

And with a tool of Lady Telma, who he had chosen as his priceless ally—a wrong tool, anyway—he had fought this negative leyline bluntly and unguardedly, and as much painfully.

Yeah, painfully; because it was of snafu and fiascos.

Now, was MyAngel another wrong tool? Yeah, was she?

<u>Chapter</u>*Twelve*

*T*his was in the first week of August.

Mr. Wyi Worri made sure his portmanteau was actually packed in, waved at Miss Iyebiye and went back to his seat. The sixteen-seater minibus was half filled with NYSC members from South-East zone, going back home after successful service. And you know what to expect where vibrant learned youths of different disciplines gathered. Of course, everyone would argue his field of study came first in the society. And this was exactly what happened in time prospect.

En route corps member Chimezie started; "In nature everything's connected, so we're held accountable for our past blunders. And I reason that since man created these problems, he can solve them. To cite example, air pollution has decrease in many industrialized cities."

But do such prospect glimmers of hope mean that mankind is gaining control of the situation? Mr. Wyi Worri thought. Aye, some called it the ecological footprint. He merely meant the measure of mankind's consumption of natural resources compared with earth's ability to replenish them. This footprint was drastically running a deficit—and now he was sure more than 70 percent of the inhabitants of Africa, and particularly his country Nigeria, used wood for cooking. Again this Africa had the highest population growth rate, and as a result the territories of vegetation had been stripped of trees. And painfully, these trees were not felled for capricious reasons. The overwhelming majority of these populations destroyed their own environment simply to survive.

"You see, Chimezie, with due sense of esprit de corps, I put it to you that you're living in a dream world," Mr. Wyi Worri challenged. "You know poor people take more than half of the world population, and now this majority destroys this environment simply to survive. I said you're living in a dream world because you leave the minute to take care of the hour. Resolve the problem of the minute and simply, it itself takes care of the hour naturally.

"Now, watch, in order to cook this suffered food with wood, the soil is stripped of vegetation and the bare top soil soon dries out and washes away by water. And here Nigeria we can tell with probity, it has resulted to many dangerous gully erosions, which have become phenomenon across the country. And what's the government doing to better the lives of the populace to solve this problem *man created and can solve?* Nothing! Rather the politicians of every tier of government have used the plight syndrome to enrich themselves the more in each and every dispensation." He showed his normal daft grin; "Anyway, deep chunk of economy has always been spent on them, but the people, us, me and you, have always never seen the result."

"But that's just one indicator of immense strain being placed in our environment. Another gauge is the condition of earth's ecosystem," Chi-Chi, another corps member, a lady this time, chipped in.

"That's right, my sister, the complex interaction of all organism within a natural environment," Corps member Chimezie said. "I mean, Mister Wyi Worri, both living and non-living matters. You see, Earth's resources are dwindling at alarming rate... who can bring the situation under control? This is where I come in."

If corps member Chimezie meant the over-all health of these

ecosystems in essence—maybe, revealed by the number of not just forest but fresh water, he, Mr. Wyi Worri, would wait and know what he would now say about it. Of course, he knew that man inhumanity to man spoke the loudest destruction of the ecosystem. Yeah, argument—he would do it today!

Auto pollution and burning were a cause for concern, they sang on radio prominently, and this was of course what corps member Chimezie believed frantically. It was good to take cognizance and agitate like he did, but could global environment be saved without making it an obligation and patriotic service in doing what the people in public positions should rightly be doing?

"Anyway," Corps member Chimezie was saying; "I was saying before Mister Wyi Worri diverted us to some other indicator, that levels of chlorofluorocarbons in the atmosphere have at last begun to decline. Atmospheric chlorofluorocarbons damage earth's protective ozone layer, and before now the quantity of them present in the upper atmosphere steadily increased, that this year's hole in the ozone layer over Antarctica reached nearly twenty nine million square kilometres."

"Indeed Earth planet could be saved if people like brother Chimezie here, who really want to save it, would think of solution beyond the short-sighted level and contest he was seeing it," Mr. Wyi Worri said. "Our battered Earth, if humans are to be held accountable for the past blunders, he should be productively considering the particular blunders that lead to destructive wars across the years. Unwholesome carbon-dioxide had oozed through the churlish mouths of those missiles across these horrible wars, and we're complaining of deplorable global warming. You remember history; the explosives had landed, reducing Cities of Hiroshima and Nagasaki to rubble, plus other similar cases over the wars across the world. Hadn't they constituted land degradation virulently? What of incessant terrorist attacks? Not just people, Earth planet is a victim of disaster. Should we simply call it tragic accident, the suicidal bombs that sweep through defenceless Earth indiscriminately—leaving destruction in their wake just for ideological reasons?

"Anyway, brothers and sisters, you don't solve problem with the level of thinking that creates it. With my superior thinking, the problem first is by and large, the world's greediness of inessential suzerainty. The blunders that led to the decrepit nature of the Earth planet point from the onset of the first world war, tout court." ...*But why was he crying more than the bereaved kinsmen over their death—as it had really likened to he-goat's head fallen into he-goat's bag?*

He was crying more because when the second world war came along in 1939, more African fresh-faced young men, were lopsidedly drawn in the alarming tens of millions soldiers and civilians that paid the ultimate price for that disastrous war. At least, the optimism about the future and human nature of native Africans also suffered a mortal blow.

"You know what?" Prince Williams was suggesting his first time; "My concern and our concern and the concern of every African learned young man out there, should be this thought of mine." He watched them archly. Of course, he was the oldest among them. "And this my thought comes this way; how could just three privileged people of the western world have money more than three nations of Africa put together?" He shrugged unbelievably. "Just three people from the occident? Could we just believe it is nature and fate really?"

Well, Mr. Wyi Worri had figuratively said it before now. When he said Africans were drawn lopsidedly, he meant just things like that. Sometimes he thought complacently, maybe he was anti-colonialist, because he usually asked himself this question of *'why so many poor in a world of riches?'* But it was reality. Obscene distribution of wealth! Was it really nature or fate that produced unfair jealous-prone share? Yeah, such share that resulted to the possibility of just three richest westerners wealthier than the forty eight nations of Africa combined as they say? And, now, this global prosperity was part of indecipherable great irony that manifested his anti-colonial inclination—of course, as he tried to grapple with it.

"Good food for thought, Chimezie!" Mr. Wyi Worri suddenly yelled. "You see, while many nations are enjoying prosperity, hundreds of millions of people live in abject poverty; is there any hope for the poor nations? That's the major problem of ecosystem." He grinned. "I think we're back still to where I was. Trust me, in my turn of mind, I don't just infer, I suspect wherever I perceive beguiling arrangement. Take for instance, imperialist covenant of the UN member states. Nothing less than unilateral domineering arrangement of the rich member states' gain.

"Guy, I said, is there any practical hope for the poor nations of Africa, if there's no tangible wealth for education and enlightenment of people; for less-stressed less-havoc modern farming and mechanization; for real researches for the government of the day of African nations; and for absence of subordination for all the nations of the world… removing that horrible air of dominion of rich and developed nations over the less privileged ones?"

"Now you said subordination and dominion of the rich and developed nations…" Corps member Chimezie started in regard to Mr. Wyi Worri's question; "Is there any European country still having dominion of colonialism on African countries? No, my brother! Let me tell what, Mister Wyi Worri's criticism simply promotes ignorance… and that's bit of obscurantism. The weltanschauung is myopic and has psychological implication that seems to point below status."

But Mr. Wyi Worri's deduction was not due to ignorance. It was not due to what he didn't understand; it was due to what he knew and believed. "Take a cop of this guy, I was a Government and Public Administration student, and in this discipline, perspicuous researches have uncovered the dubious foundation of international confederation, and the blind treaties on the side of the poor Africans. They gave us independence, and of course sovereignty, with the right hand, but still took it with the left hand. And now, in any context, where such functional tutelage is evident, people like me see it as fraudulently designed to exploit the less privileged ones the more, in a subtle manner. They call it UN chatters, but I know it's only a guise." He budged unnecessarily. "Yeah, a guise."

Corps member Chemezie grinned and said; "You said again less-privileged ones, are African states less-privileged really? Your idea Wyi Worri is rather quixotic, and has extra-prestigious implication. Let's take for instance, Nigeria as a point of view; is our country less privileged in truth? With all these numerous envious mineral and human resources? That argument is simply not logical, brothers and sisters; though when a knowledgeable personality makes an uncharacteristic utterance, it's always difficulty knowing whether it's the product of genuine error or deliberate mischief." He laughed a big one.

Mr. Wyi Worri watched corps member Chemezie laugh at him that airily, even drawing the other corps members in the snooty sarcasm with their laughs. "No, I wasn't really talking about Nigeria particularly, or maybe the western colonialism of more than three decades now. It was purely hypothetical situation…" he was disconcerted with some rasp of chagrin. "Or maybe, idea," he added, letting go.

Mr. Wyi Worri had chosen to withdraw on that discussion, with that semi-insult. Not that he had agreed, but corps member Chemezie would not anymore understand that weltanschauung with that level of his ratiocination. Corps member Chemezie wouldn't know that in addition to his professional social science, he was a bright dynamic student of the twisted world. Anyway, corps member Chemezie was a soil scientist, he wouldn't understand that African leaders had to operate within an inert administrative system—He wouldn't.

He wouldn't understand the real impact of imperialism on the African nations. Imperialism in the manifestation guise of open-door policy. *Open-door policy?* Yeah, on an imbalanced technology, of course technology know-how. No, they really used the system to subtly take back the mickey-mouse freedom and the subsequent unhealthy sovereignty.

Mr. Wyi Worri was taught at home by his elders, that truth was—or maybe at school by his tutors, that deduction was—supposed to follow evidence wherever it leads, so willy-nilly anybody trusted his credibility in his view, it was a recreant failure on nerve to back away from something that was so strongly indicated by the evidence, simply because you think the categorical conclusion had unwelcome psychological implication on your inflated empty status. African leaders accepted poverty as predestined fate of heirloom, and maybe would only let it be fought with the reliance on the fraudulent designed mechanism.

Poverty shouldn't be an heirloom of any, and now his Africa was led by many human instigated manipulations. Who was that human? World Powers they called themselves. And they were still never willing to sincerely allow real progressive prosperous breathing space on their victims.

Corps member Chemezie denied freely the delayed effect of colonialism on Africa, but what of man inhumanity of slave trade prior to it? That tomorrow people talked was today—The ideas, efforts, brainchild of those able black men and women, who were victims and offspring of victims of imperialist power, would have long ago jumpstarted a better condition in Africa. He could have cited this to short-sighted corps member Chimezie and set reality in him, before pulling in that cowardly. The occidentals' height of development would have been barren of many dimension and facets without those sold blacks. This corps member Chimezie would have known they calculatively snatched Africans their speedy prosperity. For the occidentals themselves had realized that there were cities with tall skyscrapers today in there domains because Alexander Mills, a black man, invented elevator. They had realized too that Richard Skills, a black man, probably with progenitors from Nigeria, invented the automatic gear shift for every day cars they drove. Joseph Gamble, also a black man, invented the supper charge system for internal combustion engines. And, of course, Garreta A. Morgan, perhaps from his own age-long kindred, invented the traffic signals. Now he kept those aside, still these developed nations today could have not been using the rapid transit system, for its origin was the electric trolley; and was invented by Elbert R. Robinson, another great black man.

And who knows, as brain-drain was fellitous part of imperialism, he could find himself there tomorrow giving them the honour Nigeria would have got, by the virtue of this high-powered vocation! God forbid! There was hope for him. Once he got a good job, he would save up money on his own to sponsor his subsequent books as DVI Ltd had already taken the sponsorship of his first book, and provided the whopping sum of £4800 he had made lump sum payment of 90%. Yeah, the first top-rated book.

Chapter *Thirteen*

*I*t was a sunny morning in the month of November, approximately three months he had gone about the streets as a hopeless applicant—and something seized him like seizure now he was lying there with down-weighing thoughts; *was there really hope for youths in Nigeria?* Hope to help his revered suffocating dream? And Athena Press Limited had not responded a jot to the contract they made since the 4 months he paid at once the whole amount to cover his book publication, why? Could it be he was just a brilliant thing, presenting his work in a nigh perfect state, that there was no need to touch it? Removing the necessity of sending the edited work for his approval? Then what of the page proofs that equally needed his approval? Could it be they dimed it fit to believe he must have to accept however their experts had done it? And thus waited for the last stage of printing at the 6th month?

Gawd, could it be this, could it be that? In short, he was about to suffer depression!

But he was suffering it already. This was pure miasma of depression, yeah. He knew the depressed individual had to experience ups and downs, twists and turns of feelings. And, of course, he wouldn't wait for somebody to tell him he had gone through what it was to experience a wave of sadness. Perhaps, he was suffering from serious depression. His condition had apparently become well characterized by over whelming sadness willy-nilly he wanted to believe it. And he had been in full declination, having loss of pleasure in everyday activities, and his loss of appetite for food worsening.

Maybe bipolar disorder should really receive his trepidation. Didn't traits of his illness, from all indications, include severe mood swings that vacillated between depression and mania bipolar? *Omni*, he couldn't even survive the thought only— because he would ask his sceptic self now, *have you been haunted by thoughts of suicide?* No!

No, but he must see an expert; a diagnosis was going to be needed. Sure.

Mr. Wyi Worri was about to get out of the bed when the sound from his handset jerked him round back to the bed. He picked it there it lay over the bed.

(Do you mind? You don't deserve my sympathy at all... when you can't be manly enough and face the reality about someone you call your fiancée!) A lady's voice rebuked just like that.

Mr. Wyi Worri flushed—but this strange gossiper had a lot of intolerable sassy nerve! He waited.

(Wyi Worri, your name really?)she continued.

He noticed she said that name as if words she had seen it in English language, but, well, he let himself keep his head. "Could very well be... What?"

(Sounds kind of clodhopper that never worries that bad women send good men to early graves.)

"Horrible lecture... thanks anyway."

(No trouble. If the dumb dick has eyes for something deep and strong, except what comes decorated and glittering, he'd have spotted easily all that glitters are not gold. I'm not going to help him out anymore.) Now her voice lowered confidentially; (I was in fools-paradise in the game of love once myself, and I feel for you.)

"Horrible..."

(Then get your weakling legs into action in a hurry, before the doomful rain splashes on your face unavoidably.)

"Hurry? No girl. You watch before you leap. Maybe if you've not figured out the way I see you, you're a snoopy gossiper of horrible clandestine secret system. You're the kill; you might not really be the save you're portraying."

(*Clandestine secret system!* Sounds like men of intelligence. Don't bother tracing the caller, sweetheart; I'll walk in to you if you want to see me.)

"Good," he sounded like hypocritical tiger ready to pounce. "I want to see you."

(When your manliness sweeps into action, I swear, I'll come for you to see me.)

"You've given me the challenge... so what again?"

(Mister Wyi, the door is now shut right in your face, even though you're piteously unaware. There might not be any sense in giving a chance. They had their marriage engagement last night with a male witness from her relatives, and what I'm painstakingly portraying is a price I had to pay for feeling for someone that if I don't help, would suffer the inconsolable shock I'd been to.)

Now, this matter was a curious paradox. "They?"

(Him and your fiancée.)

"Him?"

(Double-chief, of course)

"Look, now, you can see me and talk to me."

(Sweetheart, not right this time.)

"Damn you; get your meddlesome arse down where I know!"

(Uh-uh, Mister Wyi, I said I'd walk to you when your ball of suckers eventually starts acting manly... when pretty balls have summoned gut... maybe, but not right this moment you only made a decision.)

"Then, I swear, I'll come for you wherever you hide and make these cranky calls..."

She put off the line on him.

Mr. Wyi Worri stood there staring the set he held in his hand. When he stared a pretty long time, he brought it near his face and scrolled out the numbers to the one that carried the name

'*MyAngel*' and pressed the '*send*' button. The device told him there was urgent need to buff up his account, and he mused out to it that she was the first in his *family and friends* list and so however little credit that remained would do this call.

Then on the spur of the moment he confronted MyAngel with the piece of information as good as to speak out of turn.

At first she didn't believe him when he told her. Now he added real grimly; "Never you mind how I know, MyAngel. After all, it's only yesterday, but I'll prove it to you if you want, and the witness wouldn't keep from testifying if he actually understands the dubious game you're playing there."

(I want you to prove it!) she shouted, sounding like a badly disappointed friend.

"Swear. Then I'll tell you the name of this connubial partner, and who this witness was…" now he waited then asked plaintively; "MyAngel, what's really happening about your love for me?" It was a painful question, anyway. The line was quiet. He could hear her struggling to control some emotion, like swearing under her breath. It was uncalled for, but he liked it that way. He liked her to be so damned smart he would flog her conscience. After all, it was gravely mischievous for one to send somebody to market with a bag of salt, and send a rain-maker after him—she was cruelly having his head put under the knife without being prodded.

(Just tell me one thing, Mister Wyi Worri.) She finally kept a cool head.

"Shoot."

(How would you find out?)

"Don't conclude that nobody's seeing you, just because you don't see anybody looking at you; a too right nossy-perker told me. You know good-looking men have a lot of admirers; we call them *potential lovers* but women know them as *secret rivals*… the green snake on green grass. They're mostly fallen idols, and this particular helpful honey partner called the turn right on the nose."

(The helpful honey partner got a name, Mister Wyi Worri?)

"No, not this anonymous one. They're always very careful to

even disguise their voice; trust me, this could even be a guy?"

(A guy?)

He felt her frown come over the line, and a laugh trickled out his chest. "Nah, lady, definitely not your witness; he wouldn't have betrayed you so quick, though that's what you really deserve… a damned crook like you're to me in this love race."

(Damned you, Mister Wyi Worri! I…)

"You nothing… what's really happening upon our love together, was the question?"

(That question is too offensive to ask, and too inconsequential to answer, Mister Wyi Worri.)

"You get your damn fucking mouth answering…"

He was talking, but she cut the line just the taunted way the first lady did.

Was the reality staring in his face? Mr. Wyi Worri stared at the device emptily. Then the blank space was filling in gradually. Aye, agonizingly slow. But the cover was coming off the picture. There was a little more sense to it now, but like he vowed to the first lady, he must go for her, find and prove it to himself at least.

Yeah, to himself and maybe Prince Williams.

The next moment, he had recharged and called and told Prince Williams.

(You didn't recognize the voice?)

"But I've just said that!" Mr. Wyi Worri's tone went irritably. "No, I did not recognize the voice."

(Hey, don't get riled at me!) Prince Williams cautioned. (I just don't want you to go off half-cooked, that's all.)

It infuriated Mr. Wyi Worri that Prince Williams was ready to take MyAngel's side. "I'm not asking you, chum, or anybody to go off half-cooked with me here. Keep taking side with her, I don't care. Myself, I'm, sure, following up this lead."

(When something happens, don't do anything, just think. Mister Wyi Worri, think first!" Prince Williams yelled.

"Gawd, I think… have been thinking… and to follow up this lead is what I think out, Prince Williams!" Mr. Wyi Worri snapped back.

(Might be a crank,) Prince Williams said; (that snoopy lady

caller, understand?)

"No, not a bit," Mr. Wyi Worri insisted. "Yeah, I don't know who it was, but it didn't have the characteristics of a cranky caller in a strict sense. She sounded real and obliging. And sympathetic. I believe what she has been trying to say."

(You've got no proof that such level of betrayal or marital union was going to take place,) Prince Williams stayed on it. (This could be half-cooked jerk that winds up with egg on your face all over, man.)

"Let it be, chum, let it damned winds up with egg on my face, you get man, I'll follow this lead." He cut his line.

Chapter*Fourteen*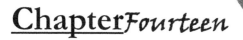

*T*he doctor picked his chart. "Yes, young man, you don't eat, and you worry too much for your future?"

"Yeah, doc," Mr. Wyi Worri conceded. "And I believe this is because I'm suffering some kind of bipolar disorder."

"Bipolar disorder?" The doctor inquired surprisingly. "Young man, that's far more serious!"

"Maybe…" Mr. Wyi Worri watched the doctor; "and please, my name is Mister Wyi Worri."

"Yes, Mister Wyi Worri… I should've known that here on your file," the doctor apologized. "Anyway, Mister Wyi Worri, your belief can't just provide a basis for making a self-diagnosis. Some of the symptoms by themselves may be symptoms of other problems besides clinical depression."

"But I experience serious depressed mood most of the day… Gawd, nearly every day, for long period now. What of the insomnia that's resulting from these feelings of inappropriate guilt and worthlessness? And this diminishing ability to concentrate anymore? Now watch me, at twenty seven, I couldn't put some flesh over my bones more than this; it's significant weight loss of so long time. Doc, what other than symptoms of major depression?"

"Of course, you might have seen them presented to serve as an overview," the doctor consented; "but those symptoms may also indicate dysthymia… a mild though more chronic form of depression. You see, you can't just have them as basis for making a risky self-diagnosis."

"Yeah, you said more chronic, doc?" Mr. Wyi Worri took from the doctor; "Well, it strikes continuously, and it's all pervasive and affects virtually every aspect of my life. It shakes me to the core."

"Jesus!" The doctor amazed. "Young man, you and your narrations!" He watched Mr. Wyi Worri in a different fashion. "But it doesn't corrode your confident or self-esteem; does it?"

"Maybe no… maybe yes… don't really know that one."

"No problem," the doctor said. "Now, what of your ability to think straight and follow decision? I mean, like you have a dream in life; how often do you harbour a recurring thought of ending it all?"

"Yo yo yo, Doc!" Mr. Wyi Worri even jubilated. "Here you hit it… it reaches so deep, and it gives a steady hard squeeze, just to tempt dangerously if you can hold on."

"Anyway, the causes of clinical depression might have answers that are not clear." The doctor was kind of backed down. "While in some cases there seems to be a genetic link, in most instances, life experience appear to play an important role. Sufferers can gain much relief by talking out their feeling with a listener like a doctor… like you think you're doing. But if you think you're actually suffering from major depression you call *bipolar*, then it must be acknowledged that when biological factors are involved, depression can't simply be willed away with a positive outlook. You may be as baffled by the condition as the sufferers do, but the dark mood of this illness you're talking about are beyond sufferer's control." The doctor took time to explain.

"Doc, I don't daftly wish myself dark mood in which I wouldn't be able to control, no," Mr. Wyi Worri said; "but I've been enduring crippling episodes of intense sadness, and world-weariness, and loss of appetite of everything… even food. A young man living… *even food!* I just go, stay and think around with empty stomach, without wishing to help it, for nowhere any metabolism works in my stomach. I have this fear that my feelings around the stomach, I tell you, doc, are blind and dead to food."

"Well, depression can take many forms," the doctor said. "Like some have what is called SAD. And SAD is seasonal affective disorder, which manifests itself during a particular time of the year. But when mania is added to the equation, the result now is called this bipolar disorder. And it's consistently inconsistent. That is, the only consistent thing about it is inconstant.

"Now, let's go; you feel you suffer disorder of bipolar during mania; can you be unbearably intrusive? And perhaps domineering? And perhaps your reckless and restless euphoria may suddenly change into rage?"

"Um… no. Not really," Mr. Wyi Worry said. "I can unbearably feel irritated about everything happening in the Globe… everything happening about global government and her administration, but not unbearably intrusive and domineering. I resign to myself. Within me they revolve, reckless and restless, and they never escape from the circle."

"Okay," the doctor said. "Now from your list, you suffer insomnia; can you really tell something you know about it… about why? You know…"

"Ah! That one is even helpful," Mr. Wyi Worri cut the doctor. "I converted it for a gain because of one dream, I often feel a great sense of power zeal, as though I could accomplish anything; so I function on a very infinitesimal sleep. And don't even bother for a nap during the day. Yet I wake up anytime with that same high energy level… like a motor running that could not be shut off. This dream is just somewhere deep inside."

The doctor waited he finally stopped his grandiose narration, and said; "How big is this dream?"

"Very big; in fact, the biggest dream of fabulous scope that really promises supernatural works of great fascination. Of course, it's got international recognition."

"That's wonderful!" the doctor ventured.

"Yeah, and to this extent, the work is packaged to add value excellently to the literary world locally, nationally and internationally."

"That's awesome... young man, very."

"Yeah, believe it, I have a publishable book that Athena Press London, has been pleased to say that her editorial department has granted their acceptance for its publication. Do you know that they actually believe it's a big novel that represents a flowering of African talent? Trust me, it's the biggest dream."

"You're a graduate of Abia State University, I guess?" The doctor now asked.

"Yeah, a local university and maybe of low standard... meanwhile," Mr. Wyi Worri rattled on; "the book and the following series would be presented flat bound, with reinforced gloss paper-book cover and full colour design. Now, who would be taller than me?"

"And the following series, you said?"

"Yeah, the subsequent novel series... like two ready so far, and four working on. I promise myself at least ten wonderful books."

"And you read literature?" The doctor wondered.

"No... not even English. I read a social science course called GPD. Do you wonder things now? Alright, my dream is all about aptitude. Talent and common sense. It's not to be born out of great acquisition of erudition."

"Well, what did you come out with?" The doctor asked again.

"Beta minus. It's unfortunate I ploughed through school," Mr. Wyi Worri said.

"Your book, who has helped in proofreading? I mean, any expert on that perspective since you wouldn't know much about literature and English?"

"Wonderfully," Mr. Wyi Worri laughed archly; "I did it myself... everything."

"And you don't wish to consult local publishers first, and you believe foreign publishers perhaps Athena Press, London, would have to grant their acceptance for their publication?"

"I said they've accepted already, with that topflight commendation."

"No problem," the doctor surrendered. "I understand your books are quite extraordinary fastidious works. Foreign publishers, like the Athena you talked, would deal only with quality works of top-rated really!"

"You've not heard, doc," Mr. Wyi Worri prat on; "Athena Press is a UK leading author funded publisher, with affiliation in USA. And for this, doc, my programme with them will be automatically promoted globally on Amazon. You know Amazon?"

"Of course… yes."

"Well, Amazon is still today the biggest marketer in the world. You know, the review notice of my books would be sent out to media worldwide, then achieving review coverage and of course, building on it by posting it on the internet."

"Alright," the doctor said at last. "Now go outside and wait. You'd be told when you'd come again to meet a psychoanalyst, for more diagnosis and counselling."

"You know I don't believe people sometimes, medication is never a sign of weakness," Mr. Wyi Worri sat put; "Don't hesitate to give me in quantum, I need my equilibrium balanced, doc."

"But medical therapy, in your case, we don't always think it this way after diagnosis."

"But it's like much the same with taking medication for other illness like diabetes, doc." Mr. Wyi Worri was just stubborn. "Balancing! Yeah, in that case, it calls for balancing of the body's nutrients. And in my own case, balancing of the brain's um… whatever; it's much the same."

"Perhaps it's much the same with taking medication for diagnosed depressive and bipolar disorder," the doctor said. "Now you have to learn not only to seek help from experts, but also to accept this help from the experts. What goes on in our mind may have much greater effect on the body than you previously believed."

"Can we simply reason away my illness with logic, doc?" Mr.

Wyi Worri insisted.

"But many people have been helped by a program of counselling that has enabled them to understand their illness. It's until you accept a help in psychoanalytic approach from a neurologist that you'd be able to stop the downward spiral. Thoughts, like emotion, affect all vital organs and systems of the human; nervous, immune, hormonal and even circulatory and reproductive."

"Please, doc, don't understand it I'm arrogant here, but giving only cognitive counselling to a depressed person of my kind status, may not attain the desired result; I pray you."

"Young man," the doctor said; "listen carefully now, I'm an expert on this, I tell you how it goes. And this is why you came. When a chemical imbalance is involved, the illness can't be simply reasoned away with logic according to you; in that case balancing the brain chemistry with a whole lot of medication is a valuable first step. Now, can you go outside and wait... every medication is poison without proper diagnosis?"

"Yes... doc."

The next day Mr. Wyi Worri came, and he was directed where he met a group of intern neurologists and of course, a lead expert.

Now he sat outside and tried to read things written on his medical file.

He read;-

(i)Psychological disorder—

Aye, they really did a good job there, trying to psychoanalyze him, even imploring psychobabble and making him reiterate the high-powered amazing task about his book project, like it was psychodrama. Yeah, he had thought in there, what a holistic psychoanalysis!

(ii) Viral wart on scalp—

Aye, that was the offensive name they found to term the off-putting congenital controversial suture of his confusing life. The phenomenon that brought to the fore the limitation of human reasoning to answer the questions of certain conundrums. He had made it a mission, but it ended up unattainable task.

He was born with the controversial scar that was believed by the entire antediluvian members of his extended families, to be the sign of his reincarnation. These members, especially the old-timers, believed his dead great grandfather came back to the world in form of him—Mind you, he promised to reincarnate with such mark as an emblematic affirmation of his reborn.

But for the sake of the little knowledge in science along his education line, the uncompromising ecclesiastic dogmas of his Christian faith, and the probity of his inclination to modernity, the circumstantial shibboleth rather was unsubstantiated and debatable.

Unsubstantiated and debatable?

But when he was involved in a ghastly road crash eight years back, and consequentially concussed into provisional death, he had transcendental experience with those horrible outer-space men. And this case became a constant confusion in his life that every moment came the indiscernible conundrum snowballed into worrisome ripple effect.

Well, he wasn't judicious about the case and hadn't loved to think about it, if not now. He had been with unfaithful disposition. Some double-standardness that wasn't healthy for the kind of Christian he caved himself for. He had made that expedient resourceful visit, and had consulted the oracle.

(iii) Malaria—

Aye, that previous doctor had listed all those malaria symptoms—and had even sent him to laboratory for a test, before visiting those neurologists.

He read down, and their further review showed features of;

(iv) Mania—

Of course this was the latest confrontation! Mania! Mania! Could this particular diagnosis tell some other things? *Mania!* Like some other strange venture of that expedient mission? Like that something that had prompted him to get to the button of the paranormals? Like the strange mystery of reincarnation, that every moment of his life came that transcendental undertaking to accomplish a mission impious?

Anyway, along the process of some quirky adventuresome journey, he had jammed an information on a clipboard that Swami Abussu gave redemptive advice and teachings on the care of man's spiritual form. And the great oracle had there admonished the people who didn't believe in reincarnation—thus she had debunked the idea of existence of hellfire unbelievably. *Wonders would never end,* she had even gone ahead to underpin the reality of astral world.

But he hadn't thought better, had he?

However, Swami Abussu had claimed of having a certain memory that she could remember dying and being born again. She was like had died, left her body and her astral form floating off, and had gone to the lower astral where it recovered from shocks and harm caused by living or dying condition on the earth.

After a few days according to earth time reckoning, she had seen all her past in the hall of memories. What she had accomplished and what she had failed to accomplish—and by assessing the successes and failures, she had decided on what had to be learnt in future she had to reincarnate. There was the existence of reborn after death; that was the iconoclastic sense she had made.

But those teachings were irreligiously boggling the mind, and she wouldn't mind! She was even smiling there as if she had won a trophy.

(v) Unrealistic Ambition—

Unrealistic Ambition, they weren't, to all intense and purposes, talking about his unrealistic mission about getting panacea to this stable confusion in his schizophrenic life. He had managed to call himself a caution to order, and then fallen back to faith in Christian God.

The psychic swami had led him to blasphemy, before he even realize it. Reincarnation in her perspective had seemed to offer a kind of apocryphal disposition in grappling with the fact of death. In this case, one head was split into two and more by the reality of reincarnation—and what of the doomsday? The infernal fire of perdition? As his religion had always believed judgment of God after death! Of course, no room for second chance!

'*This matter of hell, there's no such thing*', she had continued to narrate to him. She had debunked hellfire to mere imagination of cranky priests. Of course, there was no such thing like devil to drag one into hellfire, as no one was going to be condemned or was ever condemned. And no one was going to be sentenced to eternal damnation.

Meanwhile, those teachings there were iconoclastic to his predisposed mind. No one with psychic power like this swami, who hadn't taken notice of the reality of hell—because this thing had never been remained hidden away to people who had made for extra-terrestrial, either in deep heavy concussion or in consciousness of astral. In fact, he had considered himself fortunate to leave, and he had left stubbornly. And he had thought he had to defend his religion before her that way, particularly, since she knew well *devil exists*.

(vi) Grandiose delusions—

Delusions! Was he really confusing needs with unrealistic desire? *Unrealistic desire!* His books they were referring to? *Aw*, it was even the book they referred earlier as Unrealistic Ambition! No one had right to kill his courage. No one could chase him out of the way. Whichever, he would forgive them; they wouldn't know how much a savant he was towards that far-fetched project. They even went soft with it there—*Grandiose*. Big and impressive! His redoubtable dream!

See psychiatric clinic for assessment—

See psychiatric clinic for assessment, gracious Gawd! These lunatics themselves were all along there thinking him with mental disorder! Probably, serious! Because he wanted to press real home the magnitude of his problem, for possible redemption; or because he had a gigantic very ambitious dream a plebs of low key education background shouldn't have? He wouldn't anymore forgive them, God knows. To relate him with psychiatric problem on the basis of scurrilous sceptical substance, they were simply exercising against the ethics of their profession—fatuous dangerous envy.

Yeah, envy.
He stood and left for home.

Chapter*Fifteen*

A man in apron tagged EMS, knocked on his door, and he opened and received a moment grin from the courier service man.

"You, Wyi Worri?"

"Yeah… Mister Wyi Worri."

"Here's your parcel." The man grinned again. But this time his grin had a real touch of hero-worship. "From London."

"Thanks." Mr. Wyi Worri collected the big envelope, let a hero's grin flash across his face, signed and closed his door. He was opening it and hadn't even gone across the centre of his room, when he collapsed on the floor.

This time it wasn't just a seizure. His heart actually cracked. It cracked and received a sudden failure. And the causative parcel contained an injurious missive that was just staring the empty room brazenly.

*W*hen Mr. Wyi Worri woke up from his strange involuntary journey, he found himself back in the hospital he had so much reproached—and the same doctor that sent him to the defamatory neurologists, staring down at him.

"It's still never grandiose delusions!" he shouted, struggling to come out of the bed. "Yeah, I'm still certain about my super-impressive desire, despite that bleak prospect message there!" he shouted the more.

He was just a maniac and the hospital crew just stood watching him. Nobody should have known him with his physical description—but his purpose. And that was, trust him, the difference between his present condition and his future. Aye, it was grievously unfair to judge him with things *without*—but things *within!*

Mr. Wyi Worri jaywalked along the streets of Okigwe. He had stubbornly left the hospital that had so much misread him, once more—and was going to meet God to tell Him something confidentially, there he had once told Him some conjugal things together with his fiancée, MyAngel. Aye, he was going to remonstrate with God, but to reduce the blasphemous effect of the heresy about it, he was going to do it silently kneeling down there at the altar—just like they once did.

When he walked into this cathedral called *St. Mary's*, he met a crowd of festive people on ordination. Notwithstanding, he crossed them and headed straight to the sanctuary, the chapel, rather. He ambled into this sanctum, and kneeling before the holy tabernacle, he complained;

"God, my creator, my father," he swallowed a hard saliva; *"I'm going to say this; that You never received the doctorate degree award is not really because the scientific community has had a hard time replicating Your result, or, because some say You had Your son teach the class, or, You expelled Your first two students for learning—no, but because Your cooperative effort to Your students, God, Your creatures, have been quite limited… yeah, hardly any as it concerns me, Mister Wyi Worri, an image of You."*

He ended it that way and stood up and ambled out again.

He entered the church and sat like others, and watched as these men of God queued in the entrance procession. The thuriffer. The acolytes. The deacons for the perpetual ordination. The concelebrant priests. The monsignors. The bishops. The officiating bishops and attendants.

He waited as the homily lasted. The address of homily emphasized on religious ordination as a gift and responsibility for the sanctification of research.

But the problem with him, Mr. Wyi Worri thought irritatedly, was he had disenchantment with the church right now. In fact, he was horribly going near blasphemous with those thoughts Karl Marx had strangely hardboard. As if he had, in fact, believed religion was only opium of the masses. As if he had found truly, the cranky genius had really made a lot of circumstantial sense there, with that irreligious assertion. Of course, he had thought why God never received a PHD wasn't because of what people poorly thought He had only one major publication; or He had no references, or wasn't published in a refereed journal; or as some even doubted He wrote it by Himself. No. Far from that. They were all subjective and off-base. It was actually because His cooperative effort had been quite limited to his candidates.

Now these men to be ordained were kneeling down, and the chief celebrant was asking them questions on their readiness to devote themselves to God—and to seek perfect charity according to the constitution of the church.

The celebrant said; "My dear sons, are you resolved for this oath, with the help of God's grace, to undertake the life of believing what you read, preaching what you believe and practicing what you preach?"

Aspirant priests said in unison; "I'm so resolved."

But Mr. Wyi Worri was just seeing everything there today with unfathomable chagrin. What was this they were taking as oath? And this was the lassitude of the decay of the pulpit! Giving these men of God's vineyard impunity to put Catholic faith in reprehensive level! Brazen reprehensive level!

In that weak vow, no measure of Puritanism to check their gluttony for worldliness. No place for chastity to check against immorality.

Mr. Wyi Worri stood up. He was going to leave this place before some displeasure about life led him more irreverent about the chosen people of God.

"Brother, are you going away?" One of his neighbours there

said.

"Maybe…" he said, but then decried what was harbouring inside; "but I just can't understand why this flimsy profession! I heard, before now, the aspirant priests of Catholic Church take vow of perfect chastity, poverty and maybe obedience, which Christ our lord and His virgin mother chose for themselves, to persevere in it forever; why is this weak profession of lackadaisical call?"

"But they just resolved to believe and practice what they read, and this from holy bible."

"Yeah, I agree it mightn't be just the Conan laws. But without serious resolve against evils of flesh, they'd choose to read the history of King David and feel it's not forbidden losing your head since you can always accept your sin and ask for forgiveness."

"No, brother, these priests to be ordained are diocesan priests. That's how their vow goes. I know what you're talking about, but it's the religious priests that have theirs that puritanical way."

"Religious?"

"Yes. Religious like Missionary Fathers, Holy Ghost Fathers and congregational priests and sisters. And the monks, and the nuns… not secular or diocesan priests?"

"*Eeeehhh,* not secular or diocesan priests?" Mr. Wyi Worri mimicked stubbornly. "And these diocesan or secular priests dominate, and are the randiest. You see, putting Catholic Church in ignoble state of disrepair the Press from every mouth of the world are bashing about the candidates of Vatican city."

"Brother, they've chosen to be in the house of God and by the grace of the Holy Spirit, to spend their whole life in the generous service of God's people. They're for your sake, so watch your mouth!"

"Thank you," Mr. Wyi Worri greeted; "but don't forget that a guard of chastity would give people grim conscience… just like the vow of matrimony; that Solomon was wise, but not prudent. Period." He was moving away seriously. He was too disenchanted; he wouldn't hear any other thing those aspirants were taking in the vows. He wouldn't wait and hear that in the following answers, they resolved to give themselves to God alone, in persevering prayers and willing penance, and in humble labour and good work.

Of course they could choose to read Solomon was very generous and altruistic with his immoralities, despite his immeasurable wisdom. God knows, Mr. Wyi Worri wasn't really taking leverage of the unfortunate situation, and was now underplaying issues out of proportion. The seeming glaring lack of conformity and reverence for the ordained species, who were the highest moral authorities under the sun, didn't really bespeak of disappearing sense of religion. Just that it had decayed to unthinkable condition. The church. Catholic. Protestant. Pentecostals. All. Religion in fact. Maybe he would say it and God would understand the truth and he wouldn't be guilty of blasphemy.

Aye, the Church believed that God had done some wonderful fecund helpful thing since He created the world—He had sent his son to teach the class. Of course, to give salvation! But maybe that was only effective in the paradise. *Paradise*, mirage or utopia? No, real. But that was in the next world to come. It wasn't this dubious world now he so much lacked salvation—He cried.

The tears and bitterness congealed into hatred of worldliweariness, and the content of that let-out force majeure from London flashed into his mind, letting the heart break once more. Pathetically—

Silke & Co Ltd
Silver House—Silver Street—Doncaster—DN1 1HL

Our Ref: WTTC/IMR/PH/UR
Date: 5 December 2009

To All Known Authors

WILBURY SOLUTIONS LIMITED (FORMERLY ATHENA PRESS LIMITED) ("THE COMPANY")—IN LIQUIDATION

Dear Sir/Madam

I would advice the director of Athena instructed us to assist him in complying with the formal requirement for placing the company into creditors' voluntary liquidation.

I confirm that Ian Michael Rose of Silke & Co limited was appointed liquidator of the company at the meeting of creditors held on Tuesday 8, Dec. 2009.

Any money owed to you prior to the date of Liquidation forms your unsecured claim in the Liquidation. Unfortunately, unless further assets are discovered there will be no dividend to creditors…

Dubious world! The name of company he had contract with was even changed, and he made his payment on a fake set-up! Tears clouded his vision, he blinked his eyes to let them flow the more. No doubt about it, Mark Sykes, the Director of Athena Press LTD, knew they were having liquidation stress, even with the present company, and he went ahead and encouraged him to pay that whole mind-boggling whopping amount he loaned, in one payment, at the beginning, without taking any step into the contract! Dubious world he said—yeah.

Chapter Sixteen

$\mathcal{A}$nother December, another high days and high holidays. MyAngel had called this Friday night to announce her problem on the road. She needed his consoling words. She needed his prayer as much. The car they were coming home with broke down along Owerri—Onitsha lonely road this night. Mr. Wyi Worri had some budging indictment against her he harboured and waited like a devouring tiger, but he sagely concealed them.

There in his room, he sat secluded—looking at everything unbelievably. Anyway, it was almost bed time and he picked his pocket bible and tried to read it before night prayer.

The bible contained the mind of God and light to direct him, comfort to cheer him and perhaps food to support him. Yeah, to turn his *dis-advantage* to *this-advantage*. He would read it to be wise here. He finished one chapter and another, but they didn't do much good. He tried to think, to figure some angles and to put all things together—but nothing clicked in credible place.

Try falling in love with someone, or getting someone falling in love with you, in a clingy way sometime. Try picking up clues that trailed back some time now—like carving out a real spurious lover, without tipping your hand to some unwholesome undue scandal. He all thought.

So far it was awful. Yeah, it went terribly awry. He got spontaneous infatuation, seduced, negotiated in fools-paradise, and almost got humiliated with disrepair. It hadn't been a bad beginning. At least pale into insignificant, he knew how much underplayed he was.

Either to be used as a purposeful stopgap, or outright mockery. But why? Damn it, why the cruel mockery if he could be a failsafe to start with? That much was clear. It was better yielding to engage with him and make him real stupid in a mirage world. But why, damn it, why?

Did she use him as disrepair mockery or as a stopgap to fill her sexual desire, and then failsafe in case the causative respite turned irreparable? Either one was a reason for that oath of engagement, but which one?

He closed the bible and walked out of the house. Maybe it would be better if he should stay with old friend in distress. Maybe in a lively joint.

He turned to a phone booth and tried to call MyAngel, and couldn't get her. The next attempt got him to Prince Williams. He got all obliging when he told him it was him.

(What are you fixed? You're anxious, aren't you?) Prince Williams said.

"Nothing's amiss. I'm trying to have a think. You got any negative inkling?"

(Not really. It's about your girl?)

"How's she?"

(She surely was stranded. Call to tell me.)

"Yeah… but too bad, tomorrow's the ceremony of one year remembrance of your daddy's death we ought to attend together."

(Right… but I thought of it and send my younger brother, Lloyd, to pick her up. She has some bags of rice and other home needs.)

"Good… but too generous to pick her up that far distance. How about calling me if she arrives; think she'd love that?"

(Why, yeah…) Prince Williams slowed up a bit and added; (Sure, she needs that; she can't come home for you this night.)

*I*t was the next day, and he was en route. Presently he had statement to pick from the verse of the very Christian's charter, while a bus hauled him down to Owerri. He passed it around in his mind, and it made better sense each time; *immoral women are deadly trap; they wait for you like robbers.*

Women! His cousin, Chinonso, was among. Aye, she was right there together at the end of the wooing line, when he came into MyAngel's life. The very front end. They were inextricable, because Chinonso patted her back with equal optimism about her acceptance. They played it cordial and harmonious, and many other things, confidentially. Yeah, confidentially.

*L*ater on, a passenger's tricycle found it's legs relaxed at the open compound of Prince Williams' house—and the rider held out his hand. Mr. Wyi Worri put money in it and climbed out.

Both ladies and men of Prince Williams' guests, especially invitees, were inside the parlour. The sitting room had a television entertaining with Owerri native music. Majority of the men were doing justice to their empty bowels, and Prince Williams was yet to come to welcome him at the door.

Sitting well-nigh lonely, over the other extreme, was MyAngel. Cutesy. Beautiful comely MyAngel was in sitting position that tried to pick out her sensational taut breasts. She was a nice cute-looking dish if you hadn't got too close to the snapshot, or maybe eye-opener, to her hypocrisy—her goddamn silent subterfuge. She was watching what was showing on the TV in the manner that exposed her comeliness for some sybaritic Freudian inspection. Then her gimmick clothe, yeah; it didn't take a second look to see that if she had had some desperate sexy hot wear, it wouldn't have been more charming in the glossy world of fashion. The flared dress was rather far from being décolletage, just as her shoes were far from being flatties. Nevertheless, it was flamboyant and that gave a lot of sense of draw. The confection was tight around the waist, but it was specially designed that way to shove out the curvature of her hips

113

for some provocative display.

She saw him but wasn't exactly sure whether to get excited and rush to him, or get glum and sit put where she was sitting. His face must have made a picture of everything that went on in his mind. Maybe she would have stood for him by the next moment but Prince Williams appeared.

Prince Williams took him to the dinning side of the room, where they sat down, and his face was glimmering with good sense of warm conversation.

Not Mr. Wyi Worri.

Mr. Wyi Worri sat ramrod straight with his face averted from the besetting MyAngel, and when Prince Williams moved his lips as if to start some chat about her, he waved it off.

"What's wrong with you? I just…"

"Did I tell you I got negative inklings about her?" He waited for Prince Williams to throw a look over to MyAngel wondering, and then back to him. "Yeah, did I tell you what somebody was going to let happen on my helpless fate on the intended wedlock with her?"

"What… are you… talking about?" Prince Williams frowned at him.

"Somebody was going to exhaustibly use me as a stopgap from a failsafe," Mr. Wyi Worri said. "Somebody was going to get self-fulfilling satisfaction from blowing to my face abrasive mockery, which is tantamount with cataclysm."

"Mister Wyi Worri!" Prince Williams let out a startled grunt.

"I got tricked with that engagement oath."

"Just shut up," Prince Williams cautioned and stood to leave him. "Anyway, we'll find time later and talk this," now he sounded emollient. "Now go and see her; she's been lonely waiting for you," he charged him. "I'll bring you something to eat."

Prince Williams might be emollient but not nimble. Aye, not in the least—and Mr. Wyi Worri knew. Prince Williams wasn't a sharp ally. Mr. Wyi Worri was going to say more. The words were there in his mouth, but for his unnimbleness, they didn't come out. He flicked a glance over to MyAngel; she was watching him lugubriously. His mind was going round in cute little circumference, making mind-verification meet here and there. He was the one who caught wise in a hurry. She was a damned sharp bitch. She had nice shape and nicer air of palpable comeliness, but they were not any more drawing any potent admiration from him. He finally looked at her, trying to decide really if a lovely wench like her could play a good guy that cruel, and decided she could. A conclusive picture started to form. It was vague but with definite outline that could print an image of a murderous hypocrite. He waved her to come and started moving out.

He took her to a nearby alehouse that was as good as being empty, because of the on-going ceremony at the next compound.

"Did I ever inform you some bitch is out-using me as a stop-gap, after getting certain she has survived the vicissitude that triggered her failsafe measure? Did I ever tell you some bitch was going to get fulfilled from my piteous woe? For crying out loud, did I ever tell you it's insupportably cruel?"

MyAngel's fingers locked together. "Say it," she snapped out, her blazing eyes were nasty and wouldn't help matters; "Mister Wyi Worri."

"I was contrived into a fake engagement."

"Who?" she let out stubbornly. It was a curious mixture of emotion.

"It's not a matter of shouting," ...*bitch.* "There were a couple of things that never did make sense to me, MyAngel. They looked nice, but they really didn't make sense and I didn't give them real thought. One was that quick way I got around to engage you real. Many ladies wouldn't want a plebeian of nebulous future, of course, place a noose around their necks. You didn't put up any form of objection... even a slight one. I mean, to a guy who has only daydreams to offer.

"You hopped in this relationship on a cryptic agenda... agenda of hidden mission... mission of hypocrisy and whatever cruel mind you pre-plan. When I wanted us to take it easy, you'd had unfathomable passion you wanted every nooks and cranes of the parcels to be opened and tasted. That's something I should've thought about. You didn't think it twice to be ready to take that vow so as to force into me some libidinous desire… allowing me unto your body. Was it a good disguise… that oath? It was a damned good gimmick! Some vivacious wonderful dish making herself a cheap flirt right down to fake engagement. You, MyAngel, you."

"Not me, of course, you know," she simply denied.

Mr. Wyi Worri took his time. He expected to see horror. Real fear. He wanted to see her eyes get big as he threw the expensive indictment on her. But now he didn't know why the fear wasn't there, or why it had faded into defiance before he could even interpret it. "I was informed you were coming home with a lot of home-needs and foodstuff… the bags of rice and breakable plates; how come?"

"Why this now?"

"Answer me… you're not working anymore!"

"It was bought… someone bought them."

"Somebody bought them," he stressed. "And why?"

Those eyes got glazer if anything. "Don't be so damned suspicious and domineering. I never liked austere guys… if you're getting real austere."

"I've been austere enough. You can find that out if you want to; I mean, lady, now, if you really want to try. Some other bitches already did in my life so far."

"So now you think I planned to give you some cruel humiliation… after I might have used your naïve love to selfishly fill some stop-gap?" This was her question, though that fetching face had looked strained.

"Maybe, MyAngel, maybe. It's pretty simple when you think of it. Why else I had those warning strange dreams… like protective divine snapshots? I wrote them down in their series and can rattle them here off-hand if you want. Maybe I should throw in that suspicious negligence… the episode of that boycotted party." He watched her. "It even gets simpler. The first strange dream wouldn't have followed by another stranger dream, pointing seriously with same snapshot in making. The height of that dishonour wouldn't have come and gone with another chilling loomed up mystery that rather made good your escape.

"And now this gigantic generosity; a kind of this favour from a man who's not your husband or agitating husband-to-be, amounts to deviation and becomes reprehensible. It calls for an explanation that might not again keep your status with plaudits. And that leaves the truth. Funny, isn't it?" He grinned.

Anyway, she didn't smile. The beautiful face that strained now faded. And for the first time the day Mr. Wyi Worri saw it grew soft and tender; and if he hadn't known better, would have thought she was feeling pity and remorseful.

"Before you took notice of me and came to woo me, I'd known you and liked you," slowly she started retrospectively. "So I became your girlfriend and was besotted by your love… then I longed so much to allow free rein to my passion. And in order to boost you with greater mastery to love me better and sweeter, I allowed a matrimonial vow that rough and ready hush-hush way we did it. It was with every fibre of true love in me, and all along my dream it's the world of us as husband and wife.

"Did you ever wonder why I let myself carry your babe? I think I could tell… and as you're accusing me of fake love, I'll tell it with every bit of credence. I was never part of whoever mind, mine or another, to deride your proposal or our pre-nuptial oath. I actually thought you and I together was matching predestination. And I still think. Now, your little prayer all the time was God to give you a home and children of yours before thirty, and for this love I so much wanted to help that dream. Throwing away shame that unbelievable way, I conceived by you and for you. That wasn't enough; I was expected to abort that baby because of the danger it posed on my life, but I wouldn't dare see your seed in me get rid of. Mister Wyi Worri, I couldn't for the sake of this love. I went through hell with that pregnancy until Satan, the evil sadist, at last, got that child miscarried. Was it even miscarriage? It was stillborn at the dangerous sixth month, but upon that you were…"

"That's enough!" Mister Wyi Worri, in short, felt foolish. He didn't have to stretch his memory much backwards to hook up again with that desired thought. It was a niche for one horrible fact of remarkable interest. Unless MyAngel was the greatest natural actress that a generation of talent scouts had overlooked, or his own judgment had gone completely cockeyed, the alleged spiteful plan against him hit her with the same chilling shock-sad syndrome it had given him. He didn't call for a waiter; he went over the counter and demanded for beer himself. The way she seemed to move events to suit herself was quite counteracting, and disturbing, yeah, he felt bitter. He thought she damn well knew the score right along; his thought too labyrinthine to make sense now. A lot of pointing crazy things was going on his head, and he couldn't level them. He had thought she realized what he had come for—to make her tremble with compunction, not having the power and smartness to hark back, exploring avenues for an easy let-out. *Meen*, it weakened him. Yeah, it broke his legs and arms.

He stood there and gulped all. Instinctively he wiped his mouth with the back of his hand, and then demanded another. He went back to his seat, took a good gulp from this second bottle before he said; "Sorry, lady. I know it's a big-big mistake, but it seems in love race I never make small ones." He looked at her cowardly.

Now her eyes were levelled with his, and fire of love was in them once more. "That's okay, sweetheart." She gave a smile that said she meant it too. "That's alright, I perfectly understand."

It felt good now, and he laughed. Hell, it felt good! But, how? Felt good when you confronted and levelled charges against your wife-to-be—hot charges of double-booking her marriage, and in which yours was the fake? He meant letting you throw an in-your-face infidelity charges in her teeth, and then perfectly understood why without being sore about it even for the rest of the day?

Anyway, it was a pretty joke as MyAngel thought it crazy and was laughing too. Yeah, the idea was you could laugh off worries that you couldn't scare off with a frown.

Prince Williams walked in.

They were still laughing until Prince Williams sat down and

fixed inquisitive eyes on them. MyAngel briefly narrated him what went between them.

"You, Mister Wyi Worri!" Prince Williams spat out.

"Don't even call my name; I survived it." Mr. Wyi Worri gulped the last of his drink and wanted to call for another, when Prince Williams stopped him. He then continued; "I get in trouble a fucking lot that way. I make mistakes… big mistakes," he admitted freely.

"Maybe now you're ready to curb your uncultured inklings," Prince Williams said to him. "They're too abusive."

"Of course," MyAngel agreed readily; "or else, sweetheart, you'd get in too much to get out hardly, if you do that big mistake to the wrong people."

"Yeah, lady… to the wrong people," Mr. Wyi Worri regurgitated. But she was the wrong people? No, lady, to the right people—*for I tell you this; you're fake—you're the pure wrong people!*

Prince Williams learned close to Mr. Wyi Worri. "You're with empty stomach; you're getting drunk already… now, let's go inside the house." He stood and looked at MyAngel, who stood also.

Mr. Wyi Worri stood as much and they left.

This time don't even fear to get in trouble—she's the wrong one. The putative wrong one! Mr. Wyi Worri's ever vivid mind eye could now see MyAngel in obvious real action, as he forebodingly trudged along.

<u>Chapter</u>*Seventeen*

*I*t didn't take long MyAngel left for home the next day, the mystery driver called. With a phone pressed against his ear, Mr. Wyi Worri was pacing about restively at the back of this house they visited. He saw Prince Williams watching him the same time he was putting down back his hand, and he grabbed him on the run.

"Come and take me somewhere," Mr. Wyi Worri said. "And if you want me to tell you something, it can be while we ride."

They climbed in the hatchback Passat and waited until they had driven out into the street, before they started talking.

"Now what?" Prince Williams released the curiosity.

"Case for my suspicion. Somebody is an item."

"Who again?" Prince Williams let out yell.

"A guy that tipped me to this got his luggage mistakenly taken by my girl; he just called about it. There's a bridge of contract on love… a kind of symbiotic friendship, and his forwarding love met abysmal partnership. Now the way she and her discordant love operate, she won't give out any detail to us, for a blooming truth, unless we're right on the issue on how and where they started. She even told this man I was her brother, where I shouldn't be just a brother." Now Mr. Wyi Worri watched Prince

Williams. "What have you been up to in your silent heart, since we learned she took some stuff of the driver that drove her alone down from Lagos?"

"I was into this issue with the mistaken bag the moment Lloyd, my brother, drove her to my place and she noticed this bag that wasn't hers," Prince Williams said. His eyes drifted to Mr. Wyi Worri for a second, then went back to the road. "Were they an item… why is this unjust calumny? The bag only contains some babies' wear and kinds like that."

"*Meen,* what would they want from each other? I guess they got reason, but you just don't want to know." Mr. Wyi Worri hissed.

"Okay, she had a couple of some heavy luggage with her to take down home, and she meet him where he was taking some fuel for his car and begged him for a lift. And they had their car broken down by the way, and she called and we went for her, and that's all. They wanted to help each other."

"Help each other," Mr. Wyi Worri mused. "Each other on symbiotic thing. Man and woman, right?"

"Symbiotic, right, but a kind she had cumbersome load to haul down home from one car to another strenuously, and he needed a bubbly company to chat away the long boring journey. They were total strangers, remember?"

"So?"

Prince Williams hunched his shoulders in an emollient shrug. "So they couldn't be an item."

"Whatever contract on some love angle here, was as fallacious as my other unscrupulous negative inkling; wasn't it?

"Looks like it was," Prince Williams pooh-poohed, sailing the car through the busy track of Douglass road soberly. Up ahead was the cruciform of St. Paul's Catholic Church with the symbolic crucifix high on top, in the very manner of the crescent. He stopped, nodded genially at the gate man, and then they crossed and backed into a parking area and waited.

A pleasant sound now emanated from the cell phone Mr. Wyi Worri was purposely holding, and something like relief showed on his face, and he picked the call. "See, Mister Man, this is surely trouble; I don't know what you had with my sister, and she's picking your valuables such as babygros and things for nursing mother you bought for your sister."

(Didn't she tell you yet?)

"No, man! She didn't do anything except giving me your number and said she'd call you. See, what are you…?"

(Where's she?)

"I was just asking what you are to her…" Mr. Wyi Worri watched a little and said, anyway; "She didn't tell you when she called to give you my number? Well, Mister whatever, she's gone home and I was left behind where we attended a ceremony… she's not going to tell you. She's got reasons maybe?"

(She came to me begging for my help, and I liked her and wanted to help. She was too consummate and loveable to encounter such road *wahala* she was backing away from, and I was obliging to help with every Christian mind of Good Samaritan; you get? Well, her phone was down as she claimed, and she didn't care to reach me any way about what I bought for someone she took along. And now she left Owerri there with this gay-abandon, only to call to say she has a brother who could help to bring the bag for me, after two days had gone. But she clearly knew I wouldn't be going back to Lagos because I live in Port Harcourt. Anyway, it's not going to disturb me anymore, some young man I sent is there in the church compound. I told him to wait for you at the chapel upstairs, while he makes some prayers)

Oh, he was like denying Double chief man! "And you weren't Double chief by any means? I mean, by name Double chief?" Mr. Wyi Worri said.

(Nope; any problem on that?)

"Not really… and you said she came to you just this two days ago?"

(Yeah; any problem on that?)

"Forget it… and you haven't said something about this young man you send."

(Of course, he's tall, trim and dark in complexion. He said he's wearing a brown polo shirt. Thank you, Mister Wyi Worri.)

"Thank you… yeah, but wait a minute, um…mister what name?" Mr. Wyi Worri held him before he cut.

(Mister Richard)

"Okay, Mister Richard, you can't expect me to come along with the blooming bag, as it's away from where I was when you called. I'll know your messenger, and we'll fix how he'll pick it; understand?"

(Possibly, thank you once more.)

Mr. Wyi Worri's slacking hand swiftly went up back to his ear, and he yelled; "What's his name?"

(His name is Arum. He's probably finished saying prayers by now. Check him around the corners as well, Mister Wyi Worri.)

"Alright," Mr. Wyi Worri said and dropped the set on the dashboard, and let out a curse shudder. "Right straight to the heart… the pain. The battery of her phone was down, and she seized the let-out to severe any communication from the unneeded love… even though she was in wrong possession of someone's stuff."

"All that in one symbiotic collusion?" Prince Williams said sarcastically. "I've seen many of these love controversial misjudgements as this Mister Richard's, the driver to your girl, MyAngel. Where's the guy?"

"Waiting in the chapel," Mr. Wyi Worri grunted and opened his door. "You, wait here."

Mr. Wyi Worri got to the chapel, the young man in question was on his knees looking up about the hanging pictures of the saints—not really counting beads—and he knelt down beside him. "These Martyrs of heaven weren't really deprived and haggard, but laidback and photogenic," he said. "What do you make of that?

Arum got up with a shrug and felt his stranger's features for a moment, with the suspicious eyes he got there. "Hell, why wouldn't they? Things like this idea of yours, man, keep happening in Christendom nowadays… probably a penance angle in it." He watched him again."Yeah, the idea that the saints must undergo untold suffering and deprave themselves huge luxury to make heaven. But people with such idea aren't really observant to know who God is around forgiveness and indulgence… sanctifying zealotry, though."

Mr. Wyi Worri shrugged. "Anyway, I was going to tell you who I'm."

"I won't let you waste that air," Arum said. "I'm not even happy to see I kept you hanging around so long."

"No, man."

Almost fifteen minutes later, Mr. Wyi Worri came back and got into the car.

"What's the agreement?" Prince Williams said. "If you'd told me what we were coming for back in the house, we would have picked this bag first."

"Wouldn't love to come over to my place to pick it. Unsure safety the way just a bag thing is all going. Mister Richard was on phone again to send home a few details; MyAngel might be anything whimsical with the whole bag thing, but definitely not anything ghoulish. The young man is there doubting now. There's a couple of cryptic reasons involving but God knows, nobody knows their description."

"Not even the sceptic himself?"

"No; it's a fairly foreboding thing, and he didn't seem to get much empathy to talk over unsuccessful love affair."

"Not much of betrayal, is there any?" Prince Williams Wrinkled his Mouth. "Not for your deleterious inkling anymore?"

"I was doing a lot of thinking while I was there," Mr. Wyi Worri said; every angle he took it was a fat suspicion, nevertheless.

Prince Williams looked at him without speaking.

Mr. Wyi Worri said; "Somebody bought those mindboggling stuffs… and somebody equally gave her this wondrous lift, from Lagos, for those mindboggling stuffs!"

"Damned, some other person she went to because of heavy haulage and exorbitant fare to go about it. She needed this other help."

Mr. Wyi Worri made like he hadn't heard him, at all. "He accepted the hulking help without qualms!"

"What about it?" Prince Williams demanded impatiently.

Mr. Wyi Worri grinned at Prince Williams, then let out a short laugh. "Don't pay any attention to me, chum. Unjustified ideas, I guess. I wish I knew why the hell I harbour them expensively."

Prince Williams turned the key and started the engine. He didn't bother to back track the way they came.

Right in the heart of the town, Prince Williams said; "Huh… I almost forget; did you check your set?"

"I forget it over the dashboard here, but I came back and picked it; why?"

"Check for a massage; it rang, I'm sure, for a massage alert."

Mr. Wyi Worri scowled at Prince Williams, then brought out his phone from his side pocket. When he found a sign was dancing on the screen that a message had entered, he quickly opened the box. The top on list was a strange number as long as it wasn't stored with a name. It was stranger even with his instinct, as he had never seen or been called with. He opened the message and it was a two line sentence;-

Mr. Why 08051674301 between 5:00 and 5:30
Urgent

He pressed for option list, scrolled to *use number* and stored the number. He then extended the device to Prince Williams to see. "Could be me, couldn't it?"

Prince Williams watched for a fleeting moment. "Could be," he said, then shrugged. "However, a mistake of even one figure could send this to a wrong person. It came in just as you left for the young man. I watched it and then kept it for you to open it when you return."

"What time is now?"

Prince Williams looked at the set again. "Three o'clock, almost." He gave back the device to Mr. Wyi Worri. "And I want us to stop over for some beer?"

"Nice," Mr. Wyi Worri said.

There wasn't any trouble finding a good pub, for there were so much nice hostelries in this heart of Owerri municipal town.

The trick was finding one that had ball room to spare against boisterous revelry, as Sundays were the height of weekend fun and all that jazz.

*F*ive after five Mr. Wyi Worri told Prince Williams to order for himself more beer while he put a call. Time was still on his side, he took his time weighing for less noisy corner. Then he pointed the number and it rang once and it was a female voice again.

(Yes?)

Nevertheless, he took a brief moment to read the voice nice and deep—huh, it was controlled but suggestive. A romantic picture of what was on the other end line.

"Please I'm calling about a certain message that flipped inside the box in my phone."

(Go on.) That's the only information.

"I could be Mister Why… if it helps."

(That helps some.)

"Mister Wyi Worri is all… and it's spelt W-y-i W-o-r-r-i."

(Good, Mister Wyi Worri, you're the one.) There was a slight pause between her words. (Have you known who Double-chief is, Mister Wyi Worri? You really have to know what Double-chief is.)

Then it happened again. It was cut just like that. He didn't get it at all, but only had to go back to the bar. Across his back the little muscles were lumping up into hard knots of angry jealous; it was quite high time he followed this queer lead, for Christ sake!

However, he told Prince Williams that the massage wasn't for him after all.

*P*rince Williams had wanted another round of bottles, but Mr. Wyi Worri shook his head—satisfied for the labyrinthine day.

<u>ChapterEighteen</u>

$\mathcal{A}$day in early week of January.

Somebody wanted him to know his fate about his girl. Somebody was so altruistic to bring his head screwed hard about the detrimental fools-paradise he was swimming in piteously. Somebody who put a million worth effort to a snapshot which worked it for her now.

Mr. Wyi Worri knocked and waited for the occupant to come for the door. His thoughts were grinning at the costly pranks played by ladies. Terrible, having a couple of daft naïve men thrown themselves into fake engagements. Aye, their fake engagements—*their*, the ladies', as lived-in lovers of one lady, in the same risk of marriage thing, same trust and hope and worst, same period of time. Certain lady; this MyAngel.

What a terrible thing! This polyandry!

The strange caller was unexpectedly buxom and short, but thousands of air of amiability, and good skin of fair pigment she was bestowed with, gave her the right to make him feel like getting giddy. Before he said anything, he held on an affable urbane grin and let her buy it.

She liked it.

She showed him her sensational smile and nodded welcome. "Come in."

It was a shabby room with a couple of shabby or maybe old-fashioned chairs. Nonetheless, a dresser was at its own corner. She indicated that he should pick off the chair a couple of underwear and sit. He did just that. He threw the litters across to the place she sat on what best described as sun-lounger.

She caught them perfectly, still playing with that smile benevolently. "Call me Cyndi."

"Cyndi, you're a jovial lady!"

"Thanks." She smiled again. "So you're nosing for news… of who? MyAngel, of course?"

"You catch on quick, don't you?"

"Yes, she's the only one among my friends anybody would risk his continence for news of; you know, kind of real strange… a real beautiful player… still plays good men even at the expense of her over-ripped age of twenty five."

"Who else has been asking?"

"You, Mister Wyi?"

"Nope, sis."

"My love? You know, she saves these men with this kind of short or strange endearing names."

"I'm nobody that counts much that way; I just want information."

"Wait! Information about my friend?" She inquired unbelievably, waited, but then continued; "Okay, for twenty thousand naira, I'd stick my neck out… for half, that's ten, I know even nothing… for fifteen, maybe I'd scratch my head and scratch about."

"Sis, you can't spend twenty thousand dough of painstaking active income any better than ten or five thousand dough of easy passive income."

Her eyes glittered at him. "Maybe no, but with twenty I'd tangibly clear out my conscience. The end justifies the means, you know?"

"However, you have something about her that worth twenty thousand bucks; don't you?"

The glitter disappeared and she shouldered uncertainly. "Well, I can't even say any information about her worth twenty thousand naira to you. Maybe I'm only kidding myself since I don't even know you or what you exactly come for. It's a good long time since I put myself off from welcoming young gentlemen, who want my company for such of what I can do… and feel like talking, you know?"

Feel like talking! Talk. Small talk. Then big talk. That was all he wanted. "I saw your friend and got nuts. Then she was bare and extra-extremely beautiful. It was on this party, and I'd spent my precious time getting my proposal decorated with skilful love confession. *Phwoor,* it's nice to see her nude, and what she got about her shape up her chest there!"

She leaned forward in her chair. "I've seen her," she concurred, but that permissive air of jealousy was conspicuously felt.

"Yeah…" he saw her swallow tensely and felt good. Jealousy for her friend was all he prayed to build. It would help. "How was it?"

"Was it?—Womanly. Nice and tempting."

"Nice and tempting and I tell you, sis, I felt stupidly besotted with them." He allowed a vein to throb in his neck. "Revelry, what a damn raunchy party? I met her and we sat on our own, so my heart couldn't keep far from her charm. When I was pestering her, she was getting drunk, and the drink was going to make her throw up. Now she said her house was in the next street, and I took her home. I was still in her room when she ran into the en suit there in the room, to help her sick stomach.

"After some time, do you know what I did? I followed. Yeah, I was nervous and wanted to help, and banged into that en suit bathroom; but now she didn't have anything on, like she was about to take a quick shower. She wasn't mad at me, so my manly could hardly hold its cool. I was looking and I wanted to play, but she didn't want yet." He paused and for a moment weighed how she had absorbed that story. "How was her relationship with men… ex and current; hooked?"

"Hooked? Don't understand, bro," she intoned.

"Okay, people come around to ask for her information; It's good, many risk losing their continence, you know!"

She let out a fruity laugh. "Ever seen men played by ladies, like that of Antonia Banderas' firm *'Original Sin'*? She got them here." She watched him. "But that's unlike the guy saved with the name *'Heart'*; do you know him?"

"Heart, nope… must have loved him a great deal?"

"Yeeees—" she drawled that. "His name's actually, Richard; did she perchance discuss that with you?"

Richard! "Nope, we didn't chit-chat her relationship, after all." He watched her. "But these men keep after her cunt sheepishly, like you said? Like worshipping her, and she makes them believe she's real?"

"Maybe exactly that." She seemed less willing.

Mr. Wyi Worri tried to relax. He wished she would just feel the way he felt, and know how interesting this subject was.

"What about her other men? Maybe we talk about the one you just called *'Heart'* that went unlikely?"

"Oh, don't really count anymore!"

"Why?"

"Just an ex and must have married. He was a good looker. Handsome and debonair; so she was nuts about his magnetism. Yes, damn right she was. She was always plenty loved up about him.

"Richard was a players or something, but somehow a lover got to cheat and play around. She was still okay with that, and he knocked her off her feet with his love. Hell, she said plenty of time he tried to get her sharked up in his house. He gave her that desire. MyAngel, my friend, she liked the night bed-service treatment, so she kept herself lived-in. Then he got tired of her easy stuff, and she became a tramp. But like you admitted here, she was too okay. She got fed-up and quitted the relationship on her own. But he didn't really care."

"He had disappeared in her life, had he?" he said unsatisfactorily.

"So she said," she said even sourly. "I hope she had sense to get braced up and blew the dumb. That's what she did, I think."

Mr. Wyi Worri nodded as something was obvious there. "MyAngel didn't like that, right?"

"Pity, he treated her that way and didn't care. She was heartbroken. It was better a broken relationship than broken love, so she couldn't forget his love. He was her first love, and sometimes she wondered if she would ever love real again. So that Richard must be pretty charming... prince charming so to speak." She was smiling again. "Now you can feel it, she's just playing around. She's got a sick heart, that MyAngel, hell, fake love. You ought to see her go about these men. She makes them sympathetic and stupid. Sometimes they know; sometimes she even tell them off, walk them over, but either they're too jejune or dotty or outright cowardly, they found their knees knelling begging. She controls."

"What do you think now, sis; has she got anybody who would jump for it?"

"But you're a victim already?"

"I was, but not at that credulous height."

"No; you don't understand something here, bro. They don't just sit and trust some attitude like this. She's a damn ruthless player. To each of her victim, she plays it good... like making you think she's better be a wife... and maybe now possessively, you own her to yourself."

"Alright..." he sat forward and started almost confidentially; "I owe you five thousand naira for this cooperation... and I know I love you for this..." he grinned saucily. "Now, tell me about her current she sharks up with."

Her eyes lost their come-hither look. In a sharp level, she stared at him. "She's a player I said, she always got some lover she sharks up with."

"You know any of them, right?"

"Sure, know them all."

"Can you say a particular one? This one's the boss." He watched her then breathed to relax. He even tempted leaning back again. "Some time now, she sharks up like a wife with this one named Double-chief. Remember this one?"

She didn't talk yet. Her face was tight. And when she didn't answer right away, he showed that leering grin to remind her he would still love her for helping him.

"Well, I'm talking about the one she's had engagement of marriage with…and a witness for real confirmation?"

"Mister Wyi," she called out—slowly.

"Yeah, sis; you know I was just trying to tread on a delicate warning. Just trying to pick up pieces that'd been, anyway, perspicuous eye-opener for several months now. Just trying to find the truth behind the lead of a cranky caller about a man named Double-chief and his betrothal to my fiancée, without tipping my hand to the wrong people. I had all cautioned myself."

Cyndi nodded understandably and said; "Well, so far it was, trust me, she got you fallen head over heels in love, and she deceived you in fake marital engagement. It was a bad beginning with this her unspeakable betrayal. At least, I know how important that engagement was… that oath you took for her, you know."

"Yeah, it was so damned important she either had to be faithful or die of her conscience striking. But why, damn it, why engage to another brother, even if she must cheat on my love? That much isn't just clear!" He cursed beneath his breath. "Maybe it's common place to fuck this man for extra advantage, but why why, damn it, why another formal proposal for her hand in marriage… Consensual… Why?"

She gave a cynical snort. "You know, you've got to stop assuming that this your fiancée, MyAngel, plays by the rule. She doesn't. She considers no restrictions placed on her. Not moral, nor emotional. She sees something to her that needs doing, she does it, and she doesn't care. She has no conscience, and I tried to bring soberness to your dumb brain. She's a player. She never was real, in that sense, from the beginning."

Now he watched her. "Well, I guess it's a little wonder you didn't really care to know how I traced you down here."

She watched him too, but then smiled, pouting her lips and asking rather. "Do you have any time to spare?"

"Sure, plenty." Time wasn't that important. After this kind of revelation, probity was all he had to go by anyway. More clarification. "Nothing's due really for a couple of hours I'd board a night bus down back my home."

"I sent you warning and snapshots. You had me pretty worried, Mister Wyi; how about taking me out for a date now?"

"Fine; you're surely going to confide better."

*M*r. Wyi Worri waited her lock her door thinking; *even if there's no any further information from her, it's quite obvious she saw the binding vow as prearranged betrothal sell-out to him, Mister Wyi!*

Chapter *Nineteen*

Mr. Wyi Worri and a crook. Damned. He had blamed himself again and again, and upon again, and still again gave himself a chance to blame himself. He should have known, he kept saying each time he fought a rearguard action. He saw them all and walked into them.

En route and on night journey, amidst other passengers, he was completely with his horror thought. Yeah.

Now look.

How nice she had trapped him—aye, used him. Nobody would ever survive this. Alright he would, but he would with a battered heart. Much more. With a vulnerable broken life. A few other people would survive it, but they were rivals who were used with broken lives already.

Three years, a million starved chastity. He had come a long ponderous way to end up in cruel abject farce, with slavish credulity shamefully stretched to the limit. Maybe some lady would find a way to his heart and figure out quickly how to replace a destiny. Unlikely. Very unlikely. He wished he could know the whole story. Yeah. The whole set up before this destiny wrecker. He would like that. He would sure like to know how close he was.

He saw the angles.

Before Double-chief there was Richard, *'Heart'*, and an innocent girl, MyAngel. She was an ingénue genuine lover until the breaks got intolerable, yeah, real rough, and in a reckless abandon a vile break up came up that consequently she tied in with cynical-form of redress the balance. She played games with lover boys and picked up pleasure, and of course other alternative income, with cryptic love. Some contrived game with engagement vows throwing in as code of practice. No matter how worldly-wise these men were, it always worked for her. Yeah, always worked until she got stubborn pregnant and somebody had sense enough, and could muster suspicion, and could squawk.

For that she tried love and wanted to keep it for love, but it didn't keep her from wanting to go back in the sick game. She found the heat on the ever growing suspicion and had to abort the baby or look around for an easy conquest to operate on, and to take some responsibility. She was a clever character, she was. She found Double-chief. But she was already pregnant when she found him and didn't have any canal knowledge of him, and that could put up fat suspicion fast.

Hell, that wasn't any trouble for MyAngel. She put the squeeze on the young easy targeted searching single man named this Double-chief. He must have been pretty desperate about it. Without wasting time she bewitch-loved Double-chief into a spot that would have to protractedly henpeck him, then she brought to his notice her pregnancy, and even allowed the craving suggestion it was high time he visited her parents for the purpose of requesting her hand in marriage.

The bitch even had some insurance. She must have been fucking him from the day one she met him, until that hereditary palpable way she showed sexed love incredibly fooled him—that in the meantime he wouldn't detect the conspicuous difference in the size of three month pregnancy and that of five month. This sexed love even gunned him stupider that he could only be easy prey when she took the next step in her game. The next moment came her touching gory story she was having sudden bleeding, and finally the gory tell of losing the costly belly.

This MyAngel must be a sharp article on the guy who had the capability of bursting squawk too. Yeah, she was to him, Mr. Wyi, too. With her palpably playing her duties to her possible best to the both involved men—and convincing the restive doubting Thomas into appreciating the whole set-up she had to keep the invaluable product of love. In fact, everybody was in thrall to her—yeah, was like putty in her hands. MyAngel, she played it real cute. She found out in a hurry that if she could keep aside her ego, and possibly put away hot emotion against any of the abysmal allegations, the accuser would have to pull in his horns.

Then if eventually he didn't pull in his foreboding horns and squawked to the hearing of Double-chief, she took out another brother—and which she actually did on the sly later brazen failsafe step. Another easy conquest by the name *'My love'* was brought into the game, but she was wary enough to keep him out from the boiling incidence of the day. And it was now a weak link.

Nevertheless, the bust still came from the side of the man who had the capacity to squawk, and this agitation wind blew up the cover to the face of every partner in this—leaving the rout of fowl open for a credible candour to lay into her; but why had nobody lambasted except the man who squawked, who had done already?

Yeah, what still had to hamstring the other involved partners? *Gawd*, he wished he knew the whole backhanded set-up of his fiancée!

Mr. Wyi Worri saw MyAngel; she was coming out from the kitchen, where she was probably having her launch—her mouth was dancing with a bit of meat hanging around the corner of it, which testified what she was to be found inside doing.

He walked and sat on the resting stone placed in a corner close to the kitchen. She sauntered towards him and sat down beside him. But he didn't even look at her.

"What's up, sweetheart?" she intoned.

He didn't even want to talk to her.

"Maybe cat has got your tongue?" She stood to move away.

He looked up with a dismayed face. "MyAngel, you're too damned wanton for your own good!"

"So I've been accused, remember?"

"I'm telling you again."

"Then get some hot panties and curb me," she joked where she shouldn't have joked. "My jealous lover, do you know when you have sex with me last?"

"I keep records, for your information, not just for sex counts but many other counts. I can't bring myself to make love to you, and God saves your infected life if I run a test and have ever contacted any STD... even Chlamydia... or experience any rashes that could tell that."

She was obviously taken aback over the unexpected onslaught. "May God save me around your love!" she hissed. "I won't get flared up; your insults have lost the impart they once had, Mister Wyi Worri?" She again turned to leave.

"Stop!" he charged her.

This next desperation of him stopped her right. "What's the problem now, Mister Wyi Worri!" she heaved.

Mr. Wyi Worri watched her. Shoddy lamentation. Nothing but pure shoddy lamentation was there on her face. She was one of these adorable ladies with enchantments, like would you see in batty love ventures of Bollywood—only now she resembled a horrible woman doing the work of Delilah of holy bible in love venture of Mr. Wyi Worri. Too damn disingenuous to do anything but stare with put-on.

"I'll like to speak to you alone in my house," masterfully he demanded.

"Of all the nerve!" The lamentation made quick change into frightened suspicion.

"Right, I have that, MyAngel. I still want to level with you in private. In case you've vowed let-him-come-and-fuck-again-since-he-accused-me-of-being-infected, my room is devoid of condom and I wouldn't near you... at least not without protective. Now, do we have a deal?"

She pressed her lips together out of visible sorrow, then she hissed a curse and said stubbornly; "I don't have that time!"

His face grinned at her while the hands were making tight fists of desperation. "You can't afford to postpone this for anything in the world."

"That's your damned business," she heaved dismissively, and left walking out on him.

But he had told her he would love to take her to see his mother come tomorrow. "Stop!" he shouted, but now to a deaf ear.

Stop! He thought about that failed command worriedly, because that was always the likes of authoritative words with which he had commanding force upon people, if not that women were actually something else. Olamide, the owner of the phone line that sent him that urgent message, was brought under corporation with the commanding power of *'Don't move a muscle!'*, and it came about the link that traced to Cindy.

Olamide was an area boy, who stood at the front of a house, with one hand holding his cigarette and the other in the pocket of baggy demin jeans, when his taxi halted. Earlier now, he had settled on a fee with the driver, bought a pack of chewing gum and a newspaper to take care of his anxiety—placing the paper beside him there at the back, and tossing a piece of chewing gum into his mouth as the driver drove.

Olamide's dressing was another feature that talked everything about his street cred. When he called Olamide, leaving him with no doubt that their meeting wouldn't go by without really getting his girlfriend out of trouble that was coming after her—even as she didn't know—he knew their conversation hadn't just street value, but street culture. Anyway, Olamide was an ebony handsome guy, and he guessed him to be about seventeen. His girlfriend wouldn't be bad-looking either. Olamide was wearing a white T-shirt together with the demin jeans, while he was wearing cool brown corduroy, white shirt, and an NYSC khaki cap, and black sunglasses. He motioned to Olamide from his open window.

"Get in," he said.

Olamide threw away the stud of his cigarette and shuffled over, and climbed in. Another guy in a baggy jean was standing in the front of the house, a pretty girl, who was watching more like a girlfriend, was standing there also. That guy was a friend rather than a brother, he guessed again. Perhaps they were thinking about the whole intruding intelligence call, and this visit now. Bonhomie concern, he thought, street style.

"Want some chewing gum?" He extended the open pack to Olamide.

"No, man, me don't wan' some fuckin chewing gum. You gimme some ugly suspense." Olamide was fidgeting in his seat, tapping his feet. "And you said you're a government agent?"

"You own a phone booth; where do you operate it?"

"Me own nothing, man. True talk, me still a student."

He threw a new piece of chewing gum into his mouth and chewed them a moment, absorbing the fresh sugar. He was handling his curiosity. Olamide too tapped the pack of Benson he was holding, opened it and slid one half-way when he watched his disapproving face. He nodded *right* and said; "I'm a government agent, right, and you get to answer some questions if you need your girlfriend over there," he pointed; "out of trouble."

Olamide shrugged doubtfully. "Me don't just like this meeting… man, me don't just like you."

He didn't need a psychologist to know that. "You're in a nefarious gang, Olamide?"

"No, me not in any gang," Olamide said and looked defiantly at the government agent, blinking his eyes few seconds.

His father was once in the force, Nigerian police force; once had a theory he never forgot, that people blinked when they lied or when they were high on drugs. Might be a little of both going on here, he thought, nodded suspiciously, and gave his companion a look that would better tell him he didn't trust him since he hated him. "Tell me what you know about MyAngel, who's at the brink of putting your girlfriend into troubles with the government?"

"Me told all I know already. Me dunno nothing else."

"Tell me again," He said gruffly. "I'm stupid maybe. I can't remember."

"What," Olamide was fidgeting, sure—rubbing his hands back and forth on his trousers; "again?"

"The other lady I asked. The other lady in collaboration with MyAngel to implicate your girlfriend." One thing he was certain was that the girl standing over there, wasn't the cranky lady that was calling. And he could even bet his life, this Olamide sitting there with him, could never be the lover to the lady that had that mature sense of voice he had heard trice. At least, he had been accustomed to the voice to have authority to judge it there. "I told you she once, twice and trice called with that your phone line…"

"Me social, me likeable… me have women fans that use my fuckin line… even my sis them."

"Even your sisters?" His faculty sharpened freshly. "You said your sisters too?" That told it—maybe all. Since he was reasonably right the girl over there wouldn't be the lady in question—and Olamide couldn't possibly date the mystery caller with such superior sense, then the mystery caller was his sister—elder sister. And that was the clincher. He nodded, he was making a head. "Look, Olamide, your sister is involved here, and it'll be dangerous, I mean, real dangerous, if you don't expose her and we stop all this here and now."

"Me don't just like you," Olamide grunted.

"I know you don't like me, but here I'm to help," he said. "Now, in the evening of last gone Monday, one of your sisters used your phone to send someone a message to call her at a specific time, and he called right at that time; which of them borrowed your set at five o'clock the day before yesterday?"

"Me can't say… me have plenty sisters… me left my phone in the house."

"That person is an NYSC corps members; do you know them? And that person's called Wyi Worri… think, Olamide, think?"

"Dunno… I said me can't remember."

"Okay, sometime around June and July last year, one of your

sisters actually used your phone and made a call around eleven pm, and the person she called then called back to talk to her more, but she told you to practically tell the person she'd gone, and, in fact, it was a public phone line; do you remember?"

"Public phone line?" Olamide regurgitated.

"Yeah… and you abetted her in deception, lying to the person that your phone booth was at the streets of Lagos… Sele specifically—think."

A sudden cloud crossed Olamide's eyes, then he narrowed these eyes with strange reminiscence. "You talked a name, '*Wyi Worri*?"

"Right… Mister Wyi; you now remember?"

"Me went to Sele junction that night to see that my girl over there…" he pointed his finger; "and me met her sis too. Then we fuckin going out, and her sis made this call beside the street there. Me knew she was dodging some fuckin identity, and me remember she talked to some fellow answering some kind of stupid names." Olamide's eyes were wide with strange feelings. "She's my girl's elder sis, not me. She never asked me to make use of my phone; then me think, why you fuckin middling in my life, and fuckin connecting me with her; why? Me wan' know… man, funny, you lied."

His eyebrows arched in question. "Funny, I lied; Government agent?"

"You said here she used my phone line, man… but me never bought yet that line you lied she used."

"Yeah, I said she used the phone line that belongs to you, Olamide, but for some call not necessarily the one you know. I think she was intelligent enough to coax your girlfriend into using your phone when you weren't with it two days ago; and no how you'd know, and no one would bring you to tell me… you know."

Olamide watched him. "Me still no get any sense why you keep me here, man; me gotta leave." He reached for the door.

He grabbed Olamide's clothe tail and slapped him back against the seat. "What about taking me to her? Do you realize she was having your head put under the knife without being prodded? Take me to her place and get yourself free here… even your girlfriend too."

"Cindy is no friend of me; my girl is no even fond of her. Trust me, she's on her own. Since she needs some man to marry her, she fuckin living alone; man, she no living with the family. When me saw her that day, it was first time; me never like her." He felt the pack of cigarette in his pocket. "Gotta go." This time he flung open the car door and made it clear.

He had reached for Olamide, but Olamide was fast. He slid across the seat, knocking the packet of chewing gum to the floor board, and was almost out the door of Olamide's side when he saw him reaching for his pocket and lighting a cigarette. He now relapsed to his seat. "You're going to take us somewhere some more," he said to the driver, who had even slept only to be woken by the struggling in the car.

"But me told you me had to fuckin go!" Olamide shouted out at him.

He thrust his head and barked; "Don't move a muscle or I'll call for an arrest! Have you watched my head? What am I wearing this? I'm a corps member, and I have my primary assignment attached to the Nigerian Secret Intelligence Service called *The SSS*; do you understand? That lady you called Cindy is involved, as well involved you and your girlfriend; three counts of treason prone clandestine espionage, blackmailing and kidnapping, which contravene the laws of the land, the constitution of Federal Republic of Nigeria section 419, 420, 421 and subsection 6, 7, 8 respectively." *Fake…* "Now, are you willing to get back into the car and take me to her? I have authority to exonerate you and your girlfriend, as I have authority to draw government attention to arrest you and your girlfriend." He said he was making a head—in fact, a landmark.

He continued the questioning as they drove. He was beginning to like this issue. "So you're certain you don't know the lady, *MyAngel*?"

"How many times me gotta tell you… not a girlfriend, not a girlfriend's home-girl, not anyone, just fuckin stranger me no care to know."

"But sure you know this one, Double-Chief?"

"Me dunno any fuckin shit, man!"

"Yeah, I know you don't know him… but your girlfriend knows; don't you trust me here?"

"Me don't fuckin trust you anywhere!"

"Olamide, what you don't know is that you're my friend."

"Me don't need you; understand, man, huh?"

"That's alright; just that what you say about Cindy living alone because she needs to get married soon, made me think?"

"Think, man?" Olamide shifted uncomfortably.

"Yeah, Chum… think of maybe your girlfriend knows this man she's about to marry that rented a house for her separately, and this man maybe knows this Double-Chief… like a circle of gang."

"Dunno… me dunno… me don't fuckin know!"

<u>Chapter</u>*Twenty*

"*I* wonder this style this night!" Mr. Wyi Worri cursed.

There was every indication she wanted to sleep over in his room this night, without discarding her suit clothing—except the coat she had removed in her house before coming. She had slumped onto the bed, lying down beside him, like the USA leader and the USSR counterpart were in those days of cold war.

"What this night?" MyAngel said. "Look at me and this late night journey, I'd have slept there but I was all along thinking of you."

"You're too goddamned hypocritical!"

"So you told me yesterday."

"Gawd, I'm always telling you again."

"Then always get some nutty upset and start hitting me again." She reminded him the ineffective of his brawn approach.

Aye, he needed as well brain. Yesterday brought him the untold emotional turmoil he had never suffered like in all the frustration she had intentionally or unintentionally marooned him with her remorseless character.

If things were normal, yesterday would have been a connubial step up in their matrimonial dream. But that same fateful yesterday, to bedevil him into spiteful sorrows, she purposely left to visit someone with Betty, her friend, even before he could wake up in the morning, much more stopping her. He had suspected she left for another man's pleasure.

Anyway, she had returned at night and presented herself as a thoughtful lover, and he had dragged her to a place he had a filled day slapping hell out of her face. She didn't care to fight back, after all; she tolerated for a good number of love and respect she had for him.

"You didn't get smart this time around; did you?" he said. "That stunt you pulled, with stinking lies, that your mother would like to send you on errand to Ngookpala in Imo State? But I wonder if you ever have any relative in Ngookpala she would even want you to visit; you went for another love voyage!" he accused virulently.

"You seem to know a lot about my family," she deride that way.

He fought back a sprouted anger. "I do… about the kind of crooked love you have."

"You know about them?"

"Hell, I know about them!" His voice was a flat snarl.

"Please keep off my back, Mister Wyi Worri," she warned. "When you slapped me for a subjective canard developing from your unthinkable inklings, don't think you can do what you damn well please. Lay off my back; I never snoop about you or whatever you choose to do. Stop tracing me; you deny me every little trust and respect. You make me disgusting, keep off my back and kill me anytime I question what you do with your life."

He waited until she rattled stupidly, and now nearly whispered this; "You bitch, you know I can never be a dirty dog like you!" He slapped her face even as he lay, and waited her flared reaction, but she was studiedly tolerant. "You know it's a pointing wonder you didn't at least ask me what the doctor diagnosed about your strange ailment, on that fateful Sunday night in Ondo?"

Suddenly, she was so mad that she shouted; "I didn't have to, if you weren't curious to tell me!"

"Didn't then, but if you're the least bit interested, I didn't father any baby."

Now he noticed her teeth was making a clanking sound from some shuddering. Maybe from fear of him getting nearer the truth again, or maybe from heated annoyance over the abysmal wrongheaded angle he was taking this matter again—he couldn't fathom well, anyway.

Instead of answering his harmful assertion, she sat up and switch on the white bulb at head of the bed. She was glowering over him and wanted him to speak more to know the reason why he raised the disrespectful issue that had been buried for good long over months now.

Then something inside her told her, and her face came apart at that, and she shook with that horrible distrust.

"So you think you've got away with it?" he rasped and sat up too.

She was still shaking horribly.

"Oh, that's wrong; you didn't? Now let's talk about the unusual controversy around the baby."

She was studying him strangely; her eyes over him from face to his small shins. "I don't know what you're talking about, Mister Wyi Worri; do you know what I'll do, if you're maliciously cooking up this tawdry vile accusations?"

"Yeah, feel ashamed, fed up and finally close the door on me… small threat. Shut up and listen to me carefully! I'm going to tell you right out and you can confess it or not, but you'll be better off if you do. I never was responsible for that pregnancy, okay? So I was a sucker decidedly, and I was dumb decidedly too. I later accepted, but that was my business in the sense that I wanted to hold you with that suggestion of aborting it, but you were smarter. And then I was cooperating devotedly, thinking God would keep it and I could read the month you actually delivered, or at most I could run DNA test."

The study she was making of him now took intense petulant concentration. Every emotion she was capable of having flitted across her face until her eyes narrowed with immeasurable strange anger. "What are you exactly bringing up again, Mister Wyi Worri?"

"That you were pregnant already for some time; is that plain enough?"

"Plain enough?" she repeated incredulously."Jesuuuuus!" She didn't get it, at all. "Let me put it this way; why would I call and tell of a pregnancy that wasn't yours, when I could get rid of it easily without your knowledge?"

That question; Mr. Wyi Worri didn't know whether it armed or disarmed him rather; or should he grit his teeth and carry on, or retreat. He pulled at air soundly, and ran his hand across his face, and decided to retreat but advance in another direction. If not now, maybe next time. Then he stared unperturbedly at her. "You know, MyAngel, if you hadn't escaped that trap and later lost the pregnancy, I wouldn't even have this matter. But there was your strange ailment and the doctor's idea you were significantly pregnant in just a day stay with me, so your let-out question didn't change the matter somewhat."

"It did," she scowled out. "Nobody would ever see a reason why I should impose any pregnancy on any man who wasn't responsible, much more, one who hasn't future yet. That's a complete screw idea."

Mr. Wyi Worri had thought the same thing. A baffling indication that there was an unquestionable genuine intention. "That was disingenuous of you," he said nevertheless.

"Mister Wyi Worri, why do you think I could be having extra dubious plan?" She was suddenly cool.

Though he was real afraid to learn to that height, but he wished he could have answer to that. If he could say why, there wouldn't be a place left for her to push him over more and more. He shrugged indifferently. "I sensed it, that's all. I got instinct about it, and it's too strong. Believe it or leave."

Somewhat relaxed, she leaned back over the wall, folding her arms across her chest. "That's incredible, simply incredible and abusive. I… don't know whether to believe in your love anymore."

That's up to her, he cursed. "If… mind you, if you're denying in real truth, I certainly love to see you cleared of this on my sceptism. Until now, I had vindictive doubt about it." He grinned sagely. "But I'd made mistakes on love before, and I wasn't always fortunate to be corrected in time. MyAngel, I'll reserve my judgment until this matter comes to a head one way or another. However, I'm not relenting in settling my sight on my disposal to dredge and get the truth. Every indication I have points to your guilt. And the ones I wish I had have continued to point to the conviction of your extra-hidden agenda."

"That's your time," she chided. "But I'll tell you what, Mister Wyi Worri! I'm disappointed. Incredibly, I was broken-hearted with such level of accusation. I believed in you and your love; why all this?" It was a guilt trip question, at last. "Why, Mister Wyi Worri?" she added dolefully, and then tried to lie back still wearing her clothes. "And to tell you I'm telling the truth, I'm going to use every means at my disposal to work with you to convince you… even as you thought vindictively your indications point your blankety blank."

"You, serious!" he snide at her. "Can you give me something to start on? Maybe one good confession?"

"Maybe you try giving me a lie detector," she made that snide sarcasm. "I won't mind a bit."

"Bimbo," he hissed unsuccessfully; "that's if I got around it!"

"Yes, omnipresent!" she cursed. "You can as much be omnipotent and get around it. Won't you make sure I was guilty and knelled on the cross for unpardonable sin? Damn!"

Now Mr. Wyi Worri thought that means he was going about this wasn't the best. There could be other subtle melting yielding means. Yeah, serendipity! An inspiration came. Purely serendipitous, as he would try to seduce her into vulnerability.

Yeah, if he would raise sexual feelings in her, get her soft and sensuous, and get her gullible and contrite. If he would just do that.

Later in the night, when it was very obvious the weather was chilly, calling up little warmth; when it was certain the air was full of unheeded salacious desire, calling up romance, he tried to touch her, but met a vengeful savage scourge—

"Don't dare, you son of a bitch! You forget so soon I was

infected." The pain of his self-appointed stigma; the agony of his scurrilous distrust was traceable in her voice.

But she was fake and hypocritical! The silly impostor never was true to his sacrificial love… never in the least…

She was only wiser the more—yeah, smarter.

Chapter Twenty One

"*B*loody well, keep your body!" It was a next connubial step up; they visited his mother's station. "Blow it!" Mr. Wyi Worri hissed again.

Lights were dimmed and they were under the covers normally, but she coiled up facing the other side, and giving him her back.

He had made no effort to touch her, because he could hold his cool just about any urge, under any circumstance. He had nurtured himself to fall for sexual urge at will. He had learned how to caution his wayward cock courageously, and float his pride admiringly, while leaving the portion of inner-self feverish to that seduction.

But tonight his training failed him. He was too angry to let her get him whipped that way. Angry and... disappointed. Was that the word? *Gawd,* he breathed forbiddingly. Disappointed? Over what? His inane probability? Over his suspicion that she was infected? Well, she had sworn to hold away her sexual passion for him, that was obvious; but this was beyond the point she should give up. When would she come to the realization that it might go too risky for a partner that worth saving?

Why blooming couldn't she be a bit kinky once again? Even a dog without a tail to wag should know how to welcome its master! "Don't be such an awful punisher; why not be a little hot and bitchy for me? I mean like these models on screen that have missed their lovers?" he hissed the more.

MyAngel gave a gleeful laugh; "Oh—huh, tell me you've had that filthy dream with De Game, to fuck arse that have nasty in magazines and on screen?" She mocked heartlessly. "But that's not healthy, you know."

But she should be happy—yeah, excited instead of peevish, for he still cared enough to know how the sexuality that surrounded her affection, would still survive this long without the rightful recipient feeling them? And for a fraudulent reason she had resented his keen perception that was like he possessed an inborn lie detector that was more accurate than any one available to the law enforcement agencies? Now guilty made her defensive, as plausible explanations were harder to come by. Increasingly harder, right.

"What are you talking this?" He was implacable. "We ought to miss each other, at least!" He wasn't in real sense imitating the rapper, De Game, in his dream of fucking R and B bitches. Or when he read the article in a magazine they contained, like the rapper did, he wanted his fiancée to be exactly like hot arse. It was just that if his lady had started seeing lovemaking as an unnecessary nasty thing, then love with all intents and purposes should be seen as a questionable dull thing. "You're my fiancée, you owe me that duty."

"Mister Wyi Worri, you're in violation, let me help you understand this before we have a big problem," she said almost. "Here's a woman, not a sexpot, nor a receptacle, but a woman who clearly has her centre in herself. Your fiancée or not, this is my shaping decision and l… have… come… to it."

"But that style doesn't best communicate the insight… you know, the power and right we're brought into touch with this union. Love, which gives energy and direction to our complement and blissfulness, has lost the power to do so; maybe you never loved me," he decried.

"Maybe… if you think I'm just for sex."

"No, don't just get me that way," he debunked. "You know, I'm confused with this come up pent-up frigidity."

"Is that so?" she intoned. "Anyway, even us women, if we're honest we'll agree that we're in some way like that… a mystery to ourselves; not only to men."

"Lady, you're into it; I'm only calling like someone who aspires to be an ideal partner, to be my soul. To comfort and nurture me with the necessary love. Inspire me, seduce me. We ought to have same intuition, then I need you; allow us to feel and to relate and to listen to it. Make it sure you're the best for me."

"You know what? Sometimes I think for us women; how all the psychology about women has come from men, who call us beguilingly, *be our this, be our that.* But these are mere mental visions of women, which spring from men's needs… men's canal needs, of course."

"No, you got it all wrong; they rather spring from men's needs in their sense of incompleteness… visions which necessitated the constitution of the first union of Garden of Eden. Visions which see women as the complementary."

"Show ooo! How all too easy it is for women to be pulled in this logic. But that's not what we're just like. It's either accepting it and playing the role of man's animalistic sexual fantasies as a sex object or, Mister Wyi Worri, saying *no.* And this second alternative often seems more attractive and dignifying to me."

Caveat…this was a pointing signal. "Let me tell you, MyAngel, yeah, my lady," he said—of course, nothing again to be guarded. She was fake, and like a stopgap, she had out-used him. "Whether with your obvious withdrawn love the second alternative seems attractive or dignifying, it seriously pervades the code of love of union… complementary and clingy love of union. Take a cop of that!"

For when he was useful and needed good loving, she readily got it. If he needed it to be stoked up, she made sure she was the best for him. Yeah. She dutifully knew whatever he wanted that she was with it. And he himself knew that every woman was in her. *Gracious Gawd!*

*M*yAngel was picking her belongings when Mr. Wyi Worri woke up. There was the impression she had early in the morning swept the fenced compound, and even washed the plates to make readiness. The mark of icy Coventry was there in her attitude. He could still observe in the air, the gruff sell-out she finally dropped last night—and he felt high sense of loss of her. It saddened; very painful, nevertheless. He felt he would lose her like losing an arm, if she was gone. He had forced something about himself, to really make her different from other women. Something about him that was direct and honest to feel heartbroken, even with her apparent imposture and duplicity.

He shook the thought out of his head, and rolled out of the bed. He didn't want to feel the stupid way about the hypocrite anymore. And he didn't try to feel that way until she left the room—the house—in that incommunicado thing way, and he followed her closely behind, and then gave her only half of her transport fare back to Lagos. Why he did that was what he just couldn't tell now, only he wanted her to survive that journey scarcely. Scarcely not bountifully. Though he knew even without the half he gave, she would always survive the journey.

*A*fter Mr. Wyi Worri had had something to eat, and one or more cans of beer to hold heart, he set himself hovering over his table to put down the latest. As usual, he browsed through the earlier notes to fix sequentially the concatenation.

But this time he read en passant thinking, how he would confront this Double-chief arch rival rather—and knowing this move had backings based on circumstantial hypothesis and strange dreams, no matter how dependable and categorical. He was sweepingly taken up with the thought that he became telepathic with this Double-chief.

At least the next happening confirmed that. Mr. Wyi Worri picked his phone and a male strange voice sounded from it.

(Please sir, you're Mister Wyi?)

"Maybe, anything I can help?"

(Yeah… a great deal.) The caller swallowed conspicuously. (I'm Double-chief if you mind.)

"Double-chief… you…" Mr. Wyi Worri couldn't just stop that impulse.

(Yeah, man; but perhaps you help me this way… with this question.)

"Come on," Mr. Wyi Worri held himself.

(Mister Wyi, you're a corps member serving in Ondo State… and MyAngel, your sister?)

"Maybe she's a sister, but I was a corps member rather. Through with the National Assignment sometime around July last year."

(Okay—thank you)

Double-chief had ended that call before Mr. Wyi Worri thought if he wasn't MyAngel sister, would he have had that antagonistic primal possessive urge to protectively brag or disclose his intimacy with her.

Anyway, it wasn't so inept. The *'Maybe'* answer was a suspense worrying food for the curious mind. He would call again; he resisted the urge to call him back but stored the number.

He was closing up the today's note about five hours later when the inscription *Double-chief calling* danced on the screen of the cell phone.

"Yes… Double-chief."

(Please… um… yeah… I'm disturbed for one more thing.)

"No problem," Mr. Wyi Worri played cool.

(This MyAngel, who's a sister; how close a sister?) Double-chief paused convulsively again. (Man, I… I… mean, can someone from you marry someone from her?)

"Why blooming ask?" Mr. Wyi Worri couldn't hold out some imprecation. "Is there any fellow you know who said he's from me, and who wants to marry her, and you feel like making inquiry for him or he himself send you?"

(Nah—nah, Man.) Double-chief denied. (Just that she's my

wife, and you're this fellow, and I want really to warn you.) Automatically, Double-chief was losing his cool.

"Wait a minute! I know you're not sounding stupid?"

(Stupid…nah, man. She's my wife, and I've gone for her dowry. I've known her family for this purpose, okay?) Double-chief rattled on; (You know, I'm from far Ngookpala in Imo State, but I'll tell what here. I know all her siblings, I know her mother and I know her uncle, who stood for her late father. I know her relatives and I know all of them just for this conjugal union with her. I just called Frank Desmond, his elder brother, now, because I have expected her back to Lagos.)

Ngookpala in Imo State—Ngookpala! That name—that town— was really telling another revealing thing. *Thank you Jesus*, Mr. Wyi Worri even ventured a pray. "Look, Double-chief, it's high time you stopped being stupid. MyAngel you're talking here is my fiancée; get that!" he shouted.

(It can't be, man.)

"Well, Double-chief, we've done our little wedding there in the altar of God."

(I said, man, it can't be… who knows? Her people didn't know! The public didn't hear!)

"Alright, we actually did it in our own private way; but what matters is the presence of God there."

(Nah man, what matters is taking her people along. Mister Wyi, her people's support… their blessings! That's the tradition for picking a wife!) Double-chief was shouting his head off over there. (Now, we have their approval, they'd have their blessings on us, but we're taking our time. We want our wedding one in town. She's so beautiful and deserves high celebration, so we wouldn't hurry it… but two times we almost had it in haste, then we didn't again, then I've taken the list and would have to clear everything remaining over her dowry.)

"Then you're yet to finish the dowry, but you claimed she's your wife!"

(Yeah, she lives with me in my house, and two times I said I almost did everything… but two times we cancelled it.)

Mr. Wyi Worri was half-prepared anyway, so he said;

"Double-chief, do you like trepidation around sense of fluster?"

(That's an odd question, man.)

"And you do?"

(Nah, don't think I do, but perhaps I can manage some… in moderate dose anyway.)

"Moderate dose?"

(In short, man, I never wish trepidation around my love with MyAngel, my wife.)

"But something balefully unnerving there actually made you start worrying about me?"

"Of course, man, I have some pointing evidence worth worrying about your dalliance with my wife… that's my only fear of trepidation.) He paused, then like he had some thought he finally asked; (Why do however you ask?)

"Because, Double-chief, you're going to kick up a lot of it in a few days if you want to… unless you're the kind of a guy who jokes with his life and like Samson, marries Delilah and keeps in his house." Even if he declined by mouth which wasn't gainful, Mr. Wyi Worri knew Double-chief was dead interested in the mind.

(I… don't quite understand.)

That was Double-chief's reply, but he would. Mr. Wyi Worri would make him. "Maybe you try coming down home here one of these days, and meet this guy, Mister Wyi, over a round table. Men understand… men always understand each other over a round table, right?"

Double-chief took some thoughtful time. (Right, man; have something to take me down to Owerri in next two days… that's weekend, that's a deal.)

"Good… deal."

Mr. Wyi Worri dropped his handset over the table, but thinking; *'of course I have some pointing evidence worth worrying about your dalliance with my wife…'*

Chapter*Twenty* *Two*

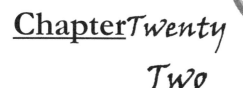

It wasn't low season, and the hotel Double-chief had his lodge was on this commercial area where public buildings were lined. It was at the heart of this town. At least Mr. Wyi Worri didn't have to fear abduction. The pub house had a spacious parking area for the teeming mobiles. His hired taxi pulled over and he left the chauffeur there, but advised him to pop in looking for him if at the end of a next thirty minutes he didn't show his face back. He went inside and had a nose around the place until he found what he wanted. The receptionist. Her small office was on the far left side of reception room.

A fat average height lady peered at him momentarily, but then pointed him to have a seat. It was dusty dry season so he expected her to throw him a rag, since he couldn't produce one and still stood. Now he demanded one;

"Yeah, I need to flick off the dust before I sit."

She didn't like that request at all, or maybe that way he did it—and she ignored that and did as if he was intolerably sassy.

"You don't expect these seats not to be a bit dirty this dry dusty session," he put again.

But this lady chose to be unwelcoming unlike what she

should have been. So she sniffed at him, but flicked a desolate handkerchief. Then the intercom rang on her desk, she listened a little and said; "He's here already." And then dropping it, she said to Mr. Wyi Worri; "Alright, Double-chief will like to see you in the conference room upstairs. And please, go straight."

Mr. Wyi Worri stood up again, but he didn't hesitate to receive her parting disapproval. She sniffed like she knew they couldn't be lovers. Maybe like the fat ones wouldn't be his interest, the lean types wouldn't dare be for her admiration.

The man Double-chief beamed at him and said; "Sit down." Then he remembered the appropriate thing to do and stood up. He gave Mr. Wyi Worri a kind of shabby shake that said he was disappointed his little rival looked too young and inconsequential, and maybe nebulous, to give him such hyper-panic tension. He was a sulky snooty guy, with an undeterred face, and an intrepid air of complacence, but you didn't have to look twice to tell that there was a lot of neurotic feelings behind the suspicious eyes that seemed to betray his self-importance. They professed he was dead interested. Taut.

"According to MyAngel, Double-chief," Mr. Wyi Worri didn't waste time to start like that—just as he got seated; "I'm a brother, a corps member who served in Ondo State, and maybe a few other things. And one doubting word you try distrustfully to find out on your own, would certainly capsize your boat of conjugal love, and put a stop to her sexual inclination to you."

Double-chief's eyebrows successfully hid a surprise.

"The name appropriately is Wyi Worri. Six months ago you checked before she could, the messages that flipped into her handset," Mr. Wyi Worri continued; "And Double-chief, you found pointing evidence… pointing evidence that balefully told another brother was trespassing with conjugal intention heavily and grounded. And you had no other option than to dare reach to this fellow against her warning—but why did it take you so long?"

The eyebrows really did nip-ups this time.

"Do you remember confronting such snapshot?" Mr. Wyi Worri said again.

"I remember."

"How do you remember the whole undignified thing, Double-chief?"

Double-chief's mode was volatile. He was obviously confused, because it was anger he seemed to be afraid was coming to surface. It was like Mr. Wyi Worri was rather a nosy nerve that needed to be put in place.

Mr. Wyi Worri said; "I'm not here after your pathetic love for her, or for unhealthy rivalry, Double-chief, so stop worrying towards that way."

Double-chief showed his teeth in a forced grin, and with that sense of double-bind he said; "I... remember the details."

"Quite clearly," Mr. Wyi Worri urged more.

"Perhaps."

Mr. Wyi Worri leaned forward confidentially; "Give your man."

"This information, man—this incidence is private, you know. And I'm sure the message thing is arguable. It could be misdirected. It could be sending to another really."

"It can't be misdirected; it can't be sending to any other where. Her name was mentioned all over the body of that message with the charges, and the damn disappointment. Maybe you were piteously henpecked with the warning she packed with good threat. She had everything to do with that vociferous jeremiad in that missive." ...*Of course, she had everything doing with that battlefield.*

Now Double-chief said; "My duty is not to prove my wife guilty, man, but to prove love and care for what we shared together. I was only with the device, helping to load it with the credit card I bought for her, when that troubling message was received and I checked it, which was normal. It truly contained complete evidence of double-booking that eventually resulted into something of seeming pregnancy. The air and tune of that message showed she had accepted the sender was responsible, but the bedfellow was painfully doubtful under the ground of same denying double-booking." He paused, watched Mr. Wyi Worri and then continued; "The outline was strange denial... but it wasn't common venture that infidelity had been exhibited in no respectful sly manner." He stopped and stared away from him a moment. "Some time ago, I had another seeming battlefield similar to yours, man. Another guy she was dating first on hidden collusions, and then it had public attention, and he started looking her up in my place. I actually picked real quarrels with her but like avowed ambition, she wasn't fazed. Sometimes this guy would meet us having quarrels over his unwarranted closeness, and she would in my presence take this guy out... and I'm sure, to a guest house, where she would reassure him her unfailing love in an illicit way. It was execrable anyway, but Hobson choice. She made a situation of incapacitating me, until she openly asked this noisome interloper not to be looking up for her."

Mr. Wyi Worri's mouth went into a sneer all by itself; "*My love*"

"That wasn't the name he was bearing."

"It wasn't? But that was the endearing name she gave him. Maybe you didn't find time this time checking her phone?"

"Alright... she managed to scare me away from her handsets. I thought you'd know about it." Double-chief's face felled. "I never thought of mentioning her indecency to you, who she called *Mister Wyi* and forbade me from reaching him. Perhaps I should have."

"No," Mr. Wyi Worri told him; "you did right. It wouldn't do good to open your mouth when she had some unnerving threat of doom of her love on you, that could turn your marriage plan upside down." He was even sarcastic, or was it sympathetic really? "I'm not condemning you; what I want is to help you kick up the caveats as you give the gory details."

Double-chief's fingers started to tap against the arm of his chair. "There wasn't really gory much to our love inclination. I met her sometime around March as a jobless applicant... a young beautiful lady that much needed the love and devotion of a young man. She was living already in this compound, before I packed in. We became friends and instantly found this new exciting clingy love. Perhaps because I became real devotional. I suggested and enrolled her for this catering course she's doing, and then I proposed for her and she was overjoyed. It was a blissful thing to a man, you know. That evening I gave her engagement ring and we celebrated it with the witness of someone from her relatives, who lives over there in Lagos. Then she found convenience and took me to see her people down home."

"Around the days of the month of June last year?"

"Three months over to be more accurate."

"You found something else, too; didn't you? Something big and heartening that happened around May… and might have made you to think whatever illicit venture she indiscriminately chose to embark on, it must have to be trifle dalliance."

A shaded surprise V formed between Double-chief's eyes. It deepened until he was squinting at Mr. Wyi Worri. "You certainly have a wealth of information about us. I did found out she was pregnant, but whether for me or not wasn't the case yet here. It was a mere unfortunate development. Actually, it was miscarried and it couldn't worth mentioning. In my opinion, however her admission of who was responsible, it took her considerable double-bluff to accept keeping the baby under the marriage agreement, but managed to relax and enjoy the glory of that love duty."

"Interesting."

Double-chief's tongue flicked over his lips. "In fact, it was easy for the underhanded love, and the contrivance, to be trusted, and they received glory. The story of a brother who calls and sends love messages, and who she visits, had to be easier balanced out.

"However, I speculated on them and arrived at the conclusion that the gory bleeding was not in true evidence, and as such, not a genuine conception. Something was taken with the intention of eventually putting up a miscarriage. Whatever was taken complicated, and it was for a scheming abortion."

"You mean a sort of having that pregnancy before that March you met her, and you thought was yours, but then it seemed some responsibility on my part played?"

"It's a case of third party we don't know here, that was successfully covered up, I guess."

"I see." Mr. Wyi Worri took an acknowledging breath, and tilted back on his chair. "You couldn't noise out your suspicion around, could you?"

Double-chief knew what Mr. Wyi Worri was getting at. The sense of double-bind crept up in his face again, and he shook his head. "Actually, I didn't see it necessary until I began to see she was making her dalliance with this other guy brazen... and I thought it over. But then that illicit trespassing was over. And again it was too scandalous to bring out around very far you talked, without absolute proof. I forgot it until I was, ah, devastated by the knowledge that she had gone to my people and trashed my earlier proposal—and I'd had a shock that bludgeoned me earlier by this corrosive message from a Mister Wyi. Then I realized that I never should have first mentioned anything about this missive to her, but under that circumstance it couldn't be helped. As you'd just suspected, she made a veiled threat if I ever reach with the subject to this controversial brother in particular, after that."

Mr. Wyi Worri shouldered in a way that said better; *then why did you dare her and bring it up now?*

Double-chief read that and it was a little pained. "I had a nagging worry about the sleazy matter ever since, and then you successfully made me look damned stupid if I wouldn't be manly to see it come out in the open now she has left for nowhere she cared to call and tell—while she told her people she was going back to Lagos."

Mr. Wyi Worri allowed himself cough up a laugh that even startled Double-chief. "Don't worry about it then," he said. "A lot of things will be out in the open for her before long, but you won't be dragged into it. You can forget the threat too. She's going to have more on her mind to nurse than trying to shaft you."

"You know where she is?"

"Yeah, I know where, but don't know who." Mr. Wyi Worri knew where she went. To a man's house, of course. "She'll turn up," he assured him, and stood up and moved, putting his hands out. "I intended this meeting to last just for thirty minutes and well," he checked his watched; "it's even gone ten minutes above it."

They shook hands again, but without much shabbily as the last time. Double-chief was watching him then said; "You can still make up your mind about it, but it'll be good if you keep this little meeting under your hat as you promised."

Mr. Wyi Worri licked his lips almost idly. "Then you'll do yourself better if you do the same too." He watched him for an indecisive moment. "And, Double-chief, if you're interested enough, the schemer supposed to be carrying my babe there in her stomach starting from January ninth last year, and she told some pathetic stories that connected to the miscarriage the same period she was telling you. And, believe me, you actually dodged telling another incident of pregnancy around the month of September same last year; because you'd planned to go and see her people for a shotgun wedding two times, and two times you'd cancelled it. If the first one was not around June I suggested and maybe that May, at least the second was approximately three months over June to be accurate. Anyway, without asking you, Double-chief, it was the same nightmarish problem that buried that one. Thanks enough." He didn't try shaking hand again, he matched out.

When Mr. Wyi Worri was about the last step, the chauffeur was coming in like being on tenterhook, but he was too late in the strict sense of such issues. And now, the diverting situation wouldn't allow him to receive a little more of hauteur from the chilly receptionist.

Mr. Wyi Worri settled the taxi man and told him to ride off. He didn't have to follow him back, though he had done his most job of raising alarm if need be. It was cloudy as weather had changed with blustery wind, but he wouldn't mind walking down the streets himself. The sky was a heavy haze building up over in the North; he could see the lines of it obscuring the sun, but wouldn't bother with the kind of conundrum he had in his brain as hell of facts.

A hell of information that danced perfect in either ways, like maddening counterweight. If MyAngel had done all the wild escapades that were alleged in the sob story Double-chief told him, and contained in his suspicion already, it meant that the story of his baby of her pregnancy was entirely fictitious. And it was hardly plausible that any man would fabricate and elaborate such a story, at a time when there was no conceivable advantage to be gained from it. But now to heck of it she needed to pretend to be pregnant for him, and take the extra risk of bringing in a phoney stillborn to build up the atmosphere. Therefore she didn't invent her pregnancy. Therefore her alibi was as good as the accusations. *As good as?* Headshake.

Was she betting that Double-chief wouldn't risk talking to him about her cynical-form identity? Good psychology, but the hell of a nerve to bet on it. Did she find out he pulled in his horn for a reason—a cryptic reason that was tantamount to lull-before-the-storm if otherwise? Then the storm would probably rock her boat and voraciously shattering it. If he saw her crush, she would expect him to feel undue sad and regret the invaluable loss that could not be restored. Dangerous. And she knew he would see her finally crush. Then why? Mr. Wyi Worri felt something like an inward explosion as he realized what his thoughts were leading to. He knew what half of his brain had never ceased to listen—searching for what instinct had scented better than reason. Yeah, on what anyone with a less optimistic flair for love adventure, things of the heart so to say, would have branded from the start as fool's errand.

He took it unaccustomed easy sauntering down the street, acting like he had the entire relaxed mind in the world at his pleasure, spending moments of mental tour getting an idea of what made his lady guilty, or maybe he himself convinced, or that Iris' apparition cocky. There were a lot of things that helped, like her unusual hunger and nasty coquetry for sex the night. Yeah, and the smart gimmicks too. Hell, there before his very eyes. People say sometimes a crook was most safe amidst his devious act and he couldn't understand that, but right in his nose—he said right in his nose—back there in Ondo state, she pulled this wool over his eyes and he didn't suspect. Or did he? Well, he did, but it was a weak type.

However there were still things that helped now, his thoughts moved on. Like her extravagant profession of love that went with dotty adulatory. Hankering. Like too ready to pledge vow of matrimony so as to be fucked. Like her complication on keeping appointments—as if some serious constraint of somewhat contract was pulling the strings.

He said here he actually did suspect and even the weak type nevertheless had a bust, and he squawked in those strident lines of message. But a smart threat on her side successfully kept Double-chief's mouth tightly henpecked, to save her face. Her face, yeah, not his face. He still wanted her to be his wife after all.

So Double-chief took out some insurance too. He filed away but close to his mouth, the incriminating words of the missive that implicated her the guy who squawked sent to her. That was the catch. He knew quite well the plaintive was only complaining and might not completely believe on what he sent—of course, he could judge that. He had succumbed to her vicious threat not to open his mouth, but not until she left him for this guy, yeah, and at one point in his insecurity, he learned that she had eloped to a place only this guy knew—and for this guy's love only.

Maybe Double-chief suspected the truth and he couldn't get her phone line, but could reach this guy's. He had picked his number and hidden it together with the incriminating words of the message, very close to his mouth. And he went ahead and opened his mouth anyway, and found out he was right, the guy wasn't the least prepared to leave her—and he had even got the costly opportunity of indivisible matrimonial vows there at the altar of God. He went disgruntled then gutted, and then nervous, and had it vomited in case some undaunted thing happened to the love this guy was having for his woman. He wasn't taking a chance on losing this bolshie angel still.

Mr. Wyi Worri nodded. Just thinking about it put everything right out where he could see them. The insurance wasn't any good to Double-chief unless he let, at this moment, this guy know what she had been up to. That way the guy couldn't afford to go on with the marriage plan. From the tone of his message, this guy wasn't going to tolerate the height of this twisted game. He had to reach this guy. Quick, too. This guy got to jilt her for him. Yeah, this guy!

Me, Mr. Wyi Worri said to himself. Yeah, him. And maybe he had made up his mind already, and it was very unnecessary to think twice about it.

M̲r. Wyi Worri woke up halfway in his sleep and couldn't go back to it again.

It was another week added and MyAngel didn't bother to call and tell where she was—as if she didn't care hell if he cared. Did he have to apologize for his feelings till eternity? Aye, did he have to feel devilishly wrong when he was evidently right— maybe keep his mouth closed like lame-brained coward?

Did he have to tell her when to care? His fiancée, how to love him? Did he have to tell her he was exquisitely lonely all this time he missed her? But he did all that. Woe, how could she claim his fiancée, but couldn't love him a single real time? As if he, Mr. Wyi Worri, hadn't figured out yet.

Well, at first it was only an abusive allegation, but now it was clear to him she would not just cheat with all her lies and freak, but murderously destroy him. Forever. Mentally, psychologically and of course, physically. One thing was certain, by the time it dawned on her she would never have a man who loved her and wished to sacrifice so much more—by the time she pulled off her dramatic pride—it would be too late.

His handset rang and he picked it.

(Mister Wyi Worri,) Double-chief's voice quavered; (she's turned up, but without atom of conscience... man, if you don't believe anything, believe she holds up her head as if...)

"Do you know that kind of man she went to?" Mr. Wyi Worri cut him.

(He's known, damn it! I talked some moments ago with her elder brother.)

"Was it an ex living in some place like Port Harcourt… married?"

(That's right,) Double-chief sounded incredulous. (His wife could be away, or he lodged MyAngel for the whole week, as nobody notices any bruise she must have got for trespassing. Trust MyAngel, her elder brother said she said it's a friend, how did you know?"

"I didn't. It just occurred to me. A couple of things just occurred to me. One is a rightful reason for seeing that a cruel hypocrite is appropriately brought to book soon… very soon." He didn't want to wait and hear more so he cut the line.

He had all the answer in his pocket, except one. The biggest one. But he got that one too. Yeah, he had got it. Know how? There was a night of a dish of aura of beauty, perceptible even in the dark bus. An alluring lady in the middle of histrionics. A soppy kind of passion. She was dead in love. Her libido crying out, hankering to douse some starved love. Her decency was to be damned. Her self-control was burnt by the excessive heat of love. It was unlikely, but it was understandable when you know crazy sex was a measure of clingy love. Her purse was found some contraceptive—almost the pills for corrosion, not prevention. It made him think of something, then a lot of things all at once, and he had all the answers, every single damned of them. He even knew how to be absolutely sure.

It was free calls all the way dawn; he picked his cell phone again.

She wasn't expecting his call, at all. She was expecting someone's and for a fraction of a second, it showed on her silence. The inability to respond immediately.

"Hello, MyAngel," he said a second time.

(Isn't this call a bit too late?) She was still a lady of pride.

When she had questioned that rudely, he kept his muteness too. No, he didn't keep mute. He let her trade with dreadful suspense and like that, his sternness resounded heavily. He never wanted to trade with malleability again. Not in a breaking point level, when the crooked game of this sort had reached a desired boiling point.

"They're all known, MyAngel; all but the biggest trick," he sounded grim confidently—as if he had pulled the real string.

(Trouble? Not here, next door.)

"Yeah, trouble... and you must face it," he admitted. He was sure this time around she wouldn't hold from collapsing under her clothes. The colour must leave her face and of course, that hard crooked heart of hers must slump. He could feel them—it was unfortunate he wasn't seeing them.

(You can't prove them, Mister Wyi Worri—you can't prove anything.)

It was too bad she wasn't able to feel, huh, read the shameful doom. "Evidence of absence is no absence of evidence, MyAngel. You actually think it'll take a lot of fruitless work to turn back the time for proper conviction, but when I'm done everybody will know what happened.

"I thought I had it a little while ago. I was ready to lay it all on some careless dalliance... expensive, of course... silently pitying this other man of love. Yeah, until I watched this man go kill-crazy and disgruntled and confessed a hell of a crooked game of a hypocritical player, who was half-known already. A gentle distinguished young man can't frustrate on mere dalliance.

"Once, Double-chief was a single still searching carefree young promising man. Soon after you came to his life, you strung him along, getting him fixed in love like entanglement, and tricked him into believing the pregnancy you were having was his. He thought he had a nice advantage there... like he was in the catbird, and dragged you into having engagement, and then to see your people for the purpose of having your hand in marriage. But you were smart enough to climb into some advancing stage in the awful prearranged game. You know, you lost the pregnancy, and so the temporary advantage would now wait at least the wound to heal.

"Too bad Double-chief forgot women of such could be deadliest. You know how the first trick swept him off his feet with nice leverage, and tried another announcement of his pregnancy the next four months. It was fake maybe, and so you have all the reason to counter announce the loss of it the next moment.

"Hell I bet Double-chief didn't even mind the credibility. He had all the intimacy he needed besides, and some wonderful lady practicing the rare dutiful wify role beyond his fantasies. A guy like Double-chief wasn't a smart partner in real dating, and mature relationship, as he was supposed to be. Hell! Something neutered his manliness and henpecked every move he made.

"No, Double-chief wasn't all that stupid; he was a clever thing too. He saw the sneaky way the beguiling love was feeding him situations, and didn't like the debatable stories that had to come and go around it. This moment a brother, who was serving at Ondo State, was calling, and the next moment you were visiting the brother, who was serving the Nation. A brother that wasn't necessary to be known by the right way, you know. And then his complicating message issue came up.

"The catch was you were undeniably guilty of adventurous illicit love and he'd known, but, Gawd, this brother wouldn't blooming be let know. What actually happened, MyAngel? Did you want to settle down with this brother and use double-chief as stopgap, but formidably Double-chief wanted things that end at the altar… and it became a catch twenty-two situation? Maybe that was why you started dating the young man you stored his name with '*My love*'. Failsafe instrument.

"Well, Double-chief was catching up to your failsafe game fast, and that tore it. He equally knew this third person was a back-up plan, and the real plan was the brother serving at Ondo State, and you wouldn't love it losing him even for the plan B.

"Double-chief made one mistake, I think. I'm willing to bet that somebody put it straight to him to watch that tailor-made pregnancy that before you could say Jack in a date, the stomach has protruded. Yeah, not even the man who was lamenting over his suspicion on his lady was responsible, but the hidden idea was blasting. It was another man that you couldn't take this stomach to. Hell! It was logical enough for his suspicion tobe noised out around, but he willingly kept his mouth shut to keep your face."

Now no how ridges wouldn't show up around that deceitful

face of hers, Mr. Wyi Worri continued; "You're a damn crook. The undeniable conviction came when you wouldn't dare want him let the brother serving in Ondo State, the real plan, know of your involvement with him... even as you've got one or two pregnancies for him. And you two had some series of hot arguments over it, in which he publicly unleashed certain accusations upon you.

"Nice motive for two-timing him; mistrust. The stupid ones supported it; didn't your brothers close their mouths when they should have cried out against such? Some that stood as witnesses during his engagement with you, approved it. It was so logical his friends encouraged him to keep a cool head and stupidly give you your head, but he was waiting watching marking time. He knew your unavoidable rapport with this third person wasn't the actual despair of him, but that which strangely distanced him from the guy you'd have loved to plight your throat with."

(The guy?) She croaked

"Yeah... me"

(You... yes,) she croaked again. (Of course, that was your pregnancy)

"Who's pregnancy?"

(You see, Mister Wyi Worri, all these stories attached to your Double-chief don't really make any meaning... logically or no logically,) she chided, untouched almost. (I didn't deny you your baby... and when you wanted us to get rid of it, I didn't ...)

"Agree..." he finished for her. "You didn't agree in getting that foetus corroded because you were on way doing it already, besides knowing I was merely suggesting that to try you. But lady, God knows, you should've been careful. You should've taken a preventive measure than curative. Some foetus are difficult; experience should've told you this. You were taking some pills already, but maybe it didn't start working like it did before, that you quickly thought the best thing was to dash the baby to this innocent gentleman, who you'd sometimes loved to settle down with... that's if you were ever going to be ready. You're a smart damn bitch, I said it before." He grinned at the devise. "You came visiting me, and you were this surprising uncontrollable nympho the night you arrived. You didn't want to delay a bit, because it could be disastrous in tagging the already pregnancy with me. I love to put things down… you knew I can easily know a nine months for a baby to arrive.

"Right, that was a pretty game. Well-arranged. Orderly. I did make love to you profusely, and still fortified for you the insurance with the same passion the following days. How many weeks have it gone before you visited? And, hell, who actually got you pregnant? I don't think it was a free young man. An ex is my choice. A certain ex who has married and wishes to be responsible to his family. You made it to hang on my head, yeah, and Double-chief got the piteous chunk of responsibility when I eventually raised alarm, because the instinctive inkling troubled my acceptance. It'd have turned out fine if Double-chief hadn't made himself an easy prey to relax your trepidation and wait for the child to eventually get washed out. The trick was successful on both of us. Hell, the kind of fibs you fed me you fed him too, and he was eventually buying. I actually bought after some persuasion in my mind… but lady, trust me, not all I could afford to buy.

"You knew that pregnancy wouldn't survive and you knew Double-chief wouldn't then know if it had been there months plus before he came into the picture. Gawd, he wouldn't know, would he?

"He wouldn't have been tricked into believing another child was forth-coming, which dangerously exposed him very susceptible to your merciless game, if not you'd allowed that engagement, and even took him to your place… what was likely to be your total succumb to his marriage proposal. Now he was out of his right brain, because the blind you had made him in love couldn't actually see and expose you without risking himself out of show, but he could keep his helpless fate alive with you by repressing whatever suspicion. It was a stalemate. Hell, a silent truce. I know you were on your damned game, you thought it a kind of gamesmanship; and I wouldn't call you a bimbo, because I know you were actually dragging yourself out of that constriction in the relationship… because simply you were in a catch twenty-two situation. *Phew*, it served right for a hypocrite of gate of hell."

Mr. Wyi Worri got up from the bed, tottered across to his table and poured himself a stiff shot from the bottle of hot there.

"Double-chief read the situation and cut himself in. Yeah, he took the advantage. He not only wanted the love, he wanted the right. The sole right. Hell, he must have thought he didn't like the boyfriend thing of friendship; he wanted the legal monopolistic thing. Unfortunately, Lady, you had a great hard time with that third guy partnership, trying to keep him under wraps. If this guy was really smart, he'd have allowed you load him with sham and keep him under cover. He wouldn't have been given the kiss off now." He grinned at the devise again. "But he didn't know about that, did he? You see, it's now he'd have helped the situation he was in the first place involved in. That brings it up to me. In one way, all these things happening since the night you visited me in Ondo were simple. Until this last mysterious disappearance, you really had people going in circle. Every one of them wanted me guilty. You made a real botch up of my love.

"Double-chief must have cursed you plenty too, MyAngel. Double-chief must curse the day he met you, because you had him by the short hair and made him to accept terms he knew that shouldn't take place. You knew right where to steer anybody... yeah. You shouldn't have lured him into marriage thing, when you had no intention of marrying him. Hell!

"I said you know where to steer everybody; MyAngel, all I want to know is why. It won't be like hating you like hell, for the rest of your life... but like hurting you like hell, for the rest of your life... and always keep the mark fresh. A child shouldn't be scared of a piece of yam his mother put in his palm, I'll like to know why. I, me, Mister Wyi Worri, was such a nice committed lover... why." ...*Because the public out there, all over the world, would be such nice people knowing why.*

She didn't answer him. His cramped hand lowered disappointedly. But he had decided, hadn't he?

Chapter *Twenty Three*

*I*n his Village, Mr. Wyi Worri lived in a rustic house amidst others. It was not just the unfair discrepancy between it and a country house, it was shared between the members of polygamous families of Dave, his grand pa. However, it was a quiet country-hood, and all houses had big compounds spacious enough to allow children play.

This country home was proximate to the country town anyway, and Prince Williams didn't have to board on a long journey to get to it. The particular house he was looking for wasn't Mr. Wyi Worri's nevertheless, but a cousin's he normally stayed to chat out moments of poignancy.

Mr. Wyi Worri was inside and spotted Prince Williams through the Window, as he confidently crossed the rustic open gate—and he came to the veranda, stopped and grinned at the old woman he saw sitting there.

"Son, can I help you?' Chinonso's mother asked of Prince Williams.

Mr. Wyi Worri and Chinonso stood to meet him, but he allowed her, the owner of the house, stepped forward ahead of him.

"Hello, can we do something for you?" Chinonso said.

"Mister Wyi Worri?" Prince Williams inquired.

She nodded at him. "That's right; it's here."

With the formal atmosphere, it was a bit hard trying to find the right start. He stepped nearer. "If he has a few minutes, I'd like to talk to him. It's pretty necessary… he knows."

Meanwhile, Mr. Wyi Worri had sat back with Betty while they waited. Prince Williams had called last time to announce a surprise visit. He had gone and met MyAngel at Lagos since she reappeared, and now had reports to tender self-appointedly. Well, Mr. Wyi Worri in preparation had told Chinonso to be around and was even fortunate, Betty, another close person to MyAngel, especially the last high days and holidays, came around.

Chinonso held the door wide open. "Certainly, come right in, Wyi Worri is waiting."

Prince Williams stepped inside and followed her into the living room. The room was orderly arranged, and you wouldn't be boosting if you say it had good taste, considering the rustic level of the country-hood or rustics making up the populates. Mr. Wyi Worri and Betty were sitting on the settee while Chinonso and Prince Williams settled themselves at the two single cushions, after he had greeted and shook hands with Mr. Wyi Worri, his friend. It was like in a round table meeting, and Prince Williams grinned and waited.

Mr. Wyi Worri watched around the three of them—him and his cousins. "I'm not a pushover, it's all about my confirmation… and she's going to pay dearly for it," he started, and he meant MyAngel that *she*.

"Confirmation?" Prince Williams intoned.

"Conviction of her fake… yeah, MyAngel."

At one time it would have incited him, but now it didn't. Prince Williams sat there interested—but there was a question in his face in prospects.

"My name is Chinonso and her name is Betty," Chinonso smiled as she contributed. "We're his cousins and as much, cousins and home girls to MyAngel."

"And as much, confederates to MyAngel," Mr. Wyi Worri supported, or otherwise chided.

"I know," Prince Williams admitted.

The ladies stared at him.

"I can't forget how your stories were going confidently prejudged, and earning unquestionable conviction?" Prince Williams continued.

"You don't seem deflated about it," Mr. Wyi Worri said suspiciously.

"Should I?" Prince Williams said.

"I was supposed to be unnecessarily deleteriously naughty."

"Deleteriously naughty?"

"To have maligned her scurrilously."

"Did you?"

Phew! Mr. Wyi Worri was more like a little boy his father was waiting to hear why he tasted the forbidden fruit from the neighbour's little daughter's thing. "No," he denied.

"Then why should I be?"

What was this guy getting to? Mr. Wyi Worri shook his head with caution. "Chum, now I don't get it."

"I never thought you were unnecessarily naughty, either," Prince Williams said.

It was real sense of discomfiture this time around, and Mr. Wyi Worri belched to customarily suppress that. He was staring at his friend, shot Chinonso a glance and then felt he had come out of it. "Let's do it over again, Prince Williams; you threw me in the fog rather." He then shot another glance at Betty. "If you thought I didn't unduly accuse her scurrilously, then why didn't you admonish her?" …Aye, Prince Williams took up the cudgels on behalf of MyAngel. He gave her the damned free rein. "Why? For he who doesn't punish evil, commands it to be done!"

"Lower your gun, Mister Wyi Worri, my friend; by the time I came to that conclusion, the chances had already gone badly delicate, that it could break the relationship I so much cherished. In all fairness to my corroborative attitude, let me say that I did admonish her on what I thought, but she didn't consider it the best. I'd weighed things, going over your doubts, suspicions, guy, carefully enough, to accept I did a hatchet job on them. Of course, I was having silent supplications."

"For what?"

"Justice. Nature, has a way of hoisting people by their own petard… especially when the victim is completely innocent," Prince Williams said.

But this sharp U-turn makes you think of misgiving contradiction, Mr. Wyi Worri thought. "Appreciated. Or maybe I remind you about her good-natured pregnancy… and her life she costly put at stake to keep my baby." Aye, Prince Williams was his main man, in fact, his confidant—*but, crippes, you don't just trust every smile you meet on the street.*

"Guy," Prince Williams grinned, and it was even a damned knowing thing; "that's one damn thing for us to figure out."

"Nice… with sacrificial love like that, on that complication she had, how would you easily figure her hurtful and devious?" Mr. Wyi Worri was damned suspicious.

Prince Williams leaned back in his chair, and somewhat his stare changed with something like touch of cautiousness. "MyAngel and I were close because of the special love I have for you. I found my conclusion right and accused her of cheating on someone who has so much put devotion around faithfulness, and who has hoped so big on her love, but she was offhanded and even laughed it off. She'd subsequently disappeared, and had admitted to me she really went to a man's place for the eight days and more. And now I tried to persuade her to call you and beg, and can even lie about her real reason of leaving your place that annoying way, but she said she's decided to leave you… and the costly union has got to the end. Do you know she was keeping a new lover? Well, she was. And a well-meant prospective husband too. A better *Mister right* after she met her waterloo that farce way you made it with your brazen knowledge of her hidden agenda with the man, Double-chief. She believed it was respectful to jilt Double-chief as well… even though he's never been willing to cancel his earlier proposal, because of her beauty.

"However, she invited me over to her place in Lagos, and coincidentally this newest Prince charming came along. He was a lawyer and co-eventually the son of her bishop in the church. Now she told me to claim her cousin, who visited from village… and I did. But she later called me and sounded as if she wouldn't expect me to mention any of them to you. The motive behind the young man's romance was to turn her a mattress with no string-attached sex, she also told me later." Now his eyes paused over Mr. Wyi Worri. "But then she confessed to me her motive for running away from you the way she did the morning she left, wasn't to hurt you or perhaps cheat on your naïve love. Far from it."

"What was it?" Mr. Wyi Worri was dead interested.

"You asked me as if I know the exact truth?"

"The day I took her to the place my mum lives and teaches, it was to show her to my mum… and then give her transport money to travel back to Lagos. Alright, in the night we had little misunderstanding about her duty to love me, but I later withdrew and let it go her spiteful way she wanted to ration her love for me. And now, in the morning, she ran. It was this morning my mum was going to formally receive her as her beloved prospect daughter in-law; what a darned disappointment!"

"Perhaps I have to go back a way to explain that for her," Prince Williams said. "She told me that firstly she ought to get her transport fare from you, but you declined from giving a complete fare back to Lagos."

"I said she ran from my house after we had some row in the night before the morning; now how would you expect me to render the full promise on the transport fare?"

"She was frightened about your spiteful behaviour, and left your place with a heavy heart that wasn't to be consoled. That may seem unusual, but it's not, according to her." Prince Williams was only a messenger here. "She received some threats and stigma from you back here in the village… and you resented her with expensive allegation of her having asexual transmitted disease.

"Anyway, she tried to put them in her tolerance bud that the whole week and more she disappeared, she actually went to see how to augment the fare back her place at Lagos."

"The heck she should run about creating avenues for some roasting, like a reckless slut!" Mr. Wyi Worri vented.

"Last time high days high holidays," Chinonso started; "maybe two weeks before she visited my cousin at Ondo state, she came home for Christmas and came to me quite concerned over some changes about her body. We're women, and when we have boyfriends we're suspicious of one thing. I suggested to her perhaps she was pregnant, and I as much offered to help her with some contraceptives. That evening when I bought the drugs for her, she was reluctant to take them… as if preoccupied with certain dreams with the baby rather. I saw her pick the two tablets, stare at them a moment, drop them and then put them away the meanwhile.

"Three months later, my cousin called from where he was serving the nation at Ondo state, and announced confidentially her conception. It seemed to excite him, and I heard him mention the words *'our perfect union'* and *'blessed union'* several times. Just between them, he went prospectively making plans for the arrival of his costly seed. And he again confided to me his plan to rent a flat for her, from his painstaking savings. In another three months when MyAngel came back home unusually at the middle of the year, I found out it wasn't with the knowledge of her fiancé, my cousin here. And, worse, she returned with another man… perhaps for her hand in marriage. It was done almost secretly, but the villagers heard, anyway. I didn't tell my cousin immediately as she's a friend. I tried to know real reasons why from her, but suspiciously she chose to distant our close relationship.

"Well, this last high days high holidays my cousin and she came back home with their earlier friendship, and the purported interest and purpose… as if nothing had happened. Not until she ran off waywardly and disappeared, and the consequent phone call from the intrusive April gentleman in question. She never told me her plans and I know they've now come against my cousin… trust me, against his innocent meaningful love. I suspected she was cheating on him decisively, but I was a confidant and she was a best friend; I couldn't do more than being a following accomplice. Who's good, after all? No one, actually! I loved her and dreamed my cousin would marry her. She's beautiful, and had vowed commitment; but not when she was so reckless to leave another man's baby… and so hypocritical to attempt to marry another man without any damn notice. And that morning, she left him with that gay abandon."

"She told me she was going to Owerri firstly, where she might stay and pass a night or two or depending," Betty now started. "However, she was going to pick some clothes or shoes she forgot there earlier before." She watched Prince Williams pointedly. "But the place she said she'd stop and pick things, wasn't it the same Owerri of your place she stopped over when she was coming home from Lagos?"

Before Prince Williams could even reply that insinuated question, Chinonso started again; "But she lied to you. I was in the same car that took her from here to Umuahia, and I could tell you she didn't join buses that go towards that direction… but Port Harcourt."

"Then if it was Port Harcourt she actually went, she lied on two things there," Betty suggested again. "She lied about the stopping and picking something at Owerri. She lied about visiting a personal friend as much." She watched them and all was waiting hungrily for her to come down. "She actually visited another guy… another aspiring husband. A cousin to me, and of course, someone I actually played the cupid. He lives in Port Harcourt, and I took her in the morning of January tenth to see the young man at home there in Ezinnachi."

The morning of January tenth to see the young man at home there in Ezinnachi! Mr. Wyi Worri's hands knotted into a fist unnecessarily. "To see the young man in Ezinnachi with her pre-informed knowledge?" He questioned Betty.

"Not actually. To be fair, she didn't really know why I requested for her to accompany me on that marital mission; but later on, she didn't feel bad about the blind date… not when we made another arrangement which she was involved." She watched Mr. Wyi Worri like reminding him. "The day before the day she went to Ngookpala, remember?" She watched all again.

"Not when she'd now secretly visited him at Port Harcourt."

"MyAngel," Prince Williams was saying; "your cousin and his fiancée, her cousin and your friend both, told me she went to stay in a different man's place. She visited Port Harcourt actually, but not to see a young unmarried man, she'd explained to me. It was a married man… and she went with sole motif of getting money. MyAngel told me God really came to her aid, as she beseeched Him on her way to the man's place; this man truly helped her and still didn't disturb her… Praise God!" he purposely joked.

They enjoyed that relief—that comic relief, except Mr. Wyi Worri. He was with another frustration. Damn, damn, damn. He was ready to catch the big bite, and it hadn't turned out simple. Her sudden rapport with Betty at the last holiday. Her sudden resentment towards Chinonso at the last holiday. Then the stubborn Ezinnachi episode that brought so much heat. MyAngel's hidden agenda, the bitch! "Betty, check this; you really played that cupid for her to get married to some cousin from your maternal place?"

"Oh! Indeed, yes."

Now Mr. Wyi Worri watched Betty; she was waiting for him to ask the next question, and it was right there—so he did. "And you didn't know she was my only love, and something ending at the altar should be our arrival?"

"I didn't know to be candid. When we were growing here in the village, when we were much younger, she had a boyfriend in her last year in secondary. A handsome boy she loved so much… and she'd never since then admitted she loved or had loved again. Richard was his name.

"But now I've noticed with remorseful mind, it wasn't entirely true she had never fallen in love again. She'd actually become a victim of love again, but never wished us to know… not when it concerns somebody, who's very close to be a cousin… not when some break-up would be doubly traumatic or rumoured… not when she's not so sure he's not bringing her out at the middle of the road, and leaving her in the shameful lurch, because relatives…relatives like me… are likely not going to be in support of this close marriage."

Aye, they say MyAngel in particular was in her previous world before her reincarnation, the big mother of Betty's grandpa—and as such Betty herself was his cousin, as her father was his father's brother, by relative of extended family. Not by consanguinity, anyway.

"Well," Betty was still saying; "I've seen where this incongruent love has come to. This incident, her secret sacrificial role nevertheless, showed me all the love that was in her heart for you. And since my disapproval was nothing but a plain subjective feeling, I couldn't help feeling sorry the way this love is now coming to an end."

"You think she was cheating with that level of impunity just because the rumour and trauma of disappointment would be doubly, because parents and relatives might not approve her marriage to me?"

"Among other things. It was gainful to have bigger better help in multi-love relationship; she needs that kind of help." Betty watched everybody once more. "Yes, that kind of help, considering the poor family… the poor widow."

"But this was not just lovers; lovers with heavy proposals," Mr. Wyi Worri reminded.

"Among other things, Good promising husband… included."

"Good promising husband… Double-chief?"

Betty nodded.

"The cousin from your maternal side?"

Betty smiled and nodded as if suggesting the guy from Ezinnachi was even the most promising.

"Hell, a whole crooked set-up!" Mr. Wyi Worri cussed. "I mean, a whole crooked set-up in a whole crooked mind!"

Betty—the smile still on her lips—had even gone a little crooked, but she nodded again.

"The motif had to be a lot of things then?" Mr. Wyi Worri said.

"Anything except with outright malice aforethought. That fact was easy."

"I thought so too," Chinonso put in.

Mr. Wyi Worri watched Chinonso suspiciously. Her eyes, no, her mouth made a funny dubious arc. The face looked a little bit happy, when it wasn't the time to be happy. He looked at this cousin of his, but one time confederate of MyAngel, like a jealous boyfriend that knew his girlfriend was telling a lie, but was waiting for her to say so first. But she had said it anyway—

Yeah, she had said it, but he had known she would, for he had said she was right there together like a co-conspirator on the end of the wooing line, when he came into MyAngel's life. He had said they were inextricable, and Chinonso had patted her back with the same counterfeit optimism. He had said they played it cordial and harmonious, and many other things, confidentially. Aye, she had been in support until one became unfathomably inimical, and abrasively suspicious. Of course, Chinonso became—after such level of fraternization and confederate role. And now she had realized that betrayal, and was bound to protect her friend back.

It was a pity; Mr. Wyi Worri turned his cautionary eyes at Prince Williams, and that must have made him uncomfortable, because he stood up and moved and nudged him to stand as well. "I don't think so too," Prince Williams replied. "I mean, it's been a horrible thing along love path... along trusting love path."

"I don't know for you sir," Betty started again, without minding the men's cold feelings. "If there's anything else, you let us know." She referred to Prince Williams. "Wyi Worri here knows we mean good for him."

"No, problem—beautiful lady." Prince Williams grinned, and took that little time to ogle Betty.

Chinonso didn't say anything, but she stood up and took the two men to the door—and then said good-bye to Prince Williams.

*F*or a few minutes Mr. Wyi Worri didn't involve in any conversation, but allowed himself follow the walk down the road Prince Williams would thumb a car. He just let it go through his head, finding a place to put real courage. He needed his manhood—*his manhood.*

"What do you think… really?" He said to Prince Williams.

"Strange lady." Prince Williams kept his face front. "Strange but horrible. Twisted. I wonder how I'd feel if I were you!"

"I'm not stupid, huh?"

"No, I seem quite convinced."

"You're a brother indeed!"

Prince Williams was a brother indeed.

Chapter*Twenty Four*

*M*r. Wyi Worri was thinking there he hunched over his table, if Mr. Ill-fate didn't actually know him by name. It was a commonplace that sometimes Mr. Ill-fate would knock on your door and wait for you to tell it *there's no seat left for you*—then it would say, *don't worry, I've brought my own stool*. But in his case, never anytime like *'sometimes'*. It swept in without knocking, and never forgot to unlawfully visit with the devastating stool.

He, however, decided to stay-up with his writing this slow night, and was about to go and open his door to allow more ventilation, when the situation became telepathic. As if he was teleoperating the door, the handle came down and the door was opening. But it was following somebody's operation at the other side, because someone was standing there. And with a colossal nerve that person closed the door and shoved herself inside.

The warrior who loses his head in battle doesn't return home to tell story, they would say—but Gawd, the case was different here.

"Mister Wyi Worri," MyAngel called out and moved to him.

He wasn't easy on her. He put his hands on her soft chest and shoved her across the room. In short, back to the door. And her back slammed unto it, and she stood there unhurt as if she nevertheless expected what was happening. But she said; "Mister Wyi Worri, why is this?"

"You asked me that?" He grinned, but the grin was cruel by nature. Hell, it was over—all! Now he was even sure of the very last detail. "You asked me that?" He repeated darkly. "Then what were you thinking when you come back here?"

She pressed her hand around her shoulders, feeling it. "Maybe I was thinking things that go like the family's not a club you can easily relinquish your membership of."

Mr. Wyi Worri took his time. He watched her abandoned state, but instead she looked desirable. The room had even smelled of her fresh powder. "Like I promised you they've all known what happened, MyAngel. Double-chief, Prince Williams, Chinonso, Betty. Hell, everybody has proper conviction. It's over…all."

Maybe she had realized why that feral action; she began to tremble. She wouldn't have power to move again, he thought and continued; "I shouldn't have fought you… you thought? But I should, rightly. Yeah, rightly love and leave you with this pang of good radiance." He watched her lips get dry, and she try to lick them—but it didn't help her any. "I must have scared the hell out of you, as I pushed the panic button over your pregnancy, that day you announced it. I made a big mistake myself in thinking I'd get away with it. You know, it's no good spreading the net when the bird you want to catch is watching you. You must have known something was screwball when it didn't piss me off that you chose to keep the baby… when I rather sucked it up and went making fatherly plan for an arrival of the baby I condemned to death. You actually knew I had dead-wondered how you suddenly went broody. The baby was the key. As long as it stayed and be born, the heat stayed on you and be revealed. Anyway, you made sure it didn't stay and be born.

"I'm going to make a guess. Let's see how close I come. Mister Wyi Worri was a sucker. Two people successfully made him that, and it was seen in the evidence. He must have been if the silent love of Chrisette, and henpecked ideas of Prince

Williams, could throw some crippling resignation and amenability into him, so bad that when he even squawked around, they towered over him, wanting him to shut up and pull in his horn cowardly. But Mister Wyi Worri was a trained student of the World of Eve, and graduated with a lot of experience, so he had a reason to be dumb. Let's say he lost all his experience where it counted, and in blind love he had none left. You know, it's not hard for a woman to fool a man who's in love with her, especially if this man that loves this woman suddenly becomes this blind in a reckless way."

He saw MyAngel give out an uncontrollable in-breath that betrayed her.

"So he had questioned the time you must have taken in. Then he became cagey and wanted to wait until he saw what you're up to, but you didn't wait. You picked out a good readymade susceptible victim, and waited until you finally made his silent intention unattainable.

"That was an easy shot too. Mister Wyi Worri should've known the trick right there. You didn't leave the evidence of your ailment, the blood, in the toilet seat, and he was counting a concerned brave lady of clingy love, almost like Juliet of Shares Spares. He should've been counting a brave crook that knows so little about clingy love, and how to hold chastity and make fidelity.

"Then there was that little psycho-episode in his room, but you traced him to that spot with so much unbelievable tolerance that kept him guessing. One of the marks of maturity is the ability to disagree without becoming disagreeable, but he wasn't trying to work with a cool head and suck it up, so it must have been pretty easy for you to keep successful check on him.

"Chrisette, she was an inspiration. She was another strength that could've backed formidably the prophetic prognoses, if she'd wanted to take the chances of unmasking her true self for his love. She knew you didn't know she was fighting against some cheapening but ungovernable love she had developed for him, but he did. She didn't play benevolent honest broker out there that evening… no… rather she was trying to bridle his advances.

"MyAngel, you should've left this game of love of bond to the true players. True players like Chrisette. They're much chaste at it. Hell, it was her who was messing the prophetic divination up, in her hurry bid to get a rightful distance from him. She quickly found collaboration in Prince Williams' relation with you. She actually thought Mister Wyi Worri's heartbeat that pathetically called for her attention in form of little love, was the real problem between him and you. Lady, she just didn't know. Those melting callouts didn't have a thing to do with anything, except give him preventive alert to lay caution against your possible severance of his love. She surely came up with some choice morsel after that thought."

Some chattering smiles came across MyAngel's face rudely. She was smiling. Damn it, the bitch was catching fun daringly. She was there laughing at him, hardly moping, much more holding any fear. Mr. Wyi Worri he fought a choke, trying to continue—a damned choke. He would surely rip her inside out.

"Let's not forget Prince Williams, the great fixer, here. He might be right with his sermon about love, but I think he had weighed the dubious scenario at one time there, but he was a spent-force to do anything about it. He must have put a lot of things together, including your lastly mysterious disappearance. Well, he was full of nuts about your physical charm when this Mister Wyi Worri invited them into your world with him. By some accident, perchance, you happened to seduce him into having fawning admiration for you. Yeah, it was a slight case of eternal triangle. Prince Williams had secret harmful love for you. It had a lot of information about his henpecked approach. Damn, I say it actually had a lot of things to tell."

He breathed in soundly, and held it a moment, waiting to hear her protest against that new reckless allegation. But she didn't mind—and that he never stopped wondering why she wouldn't dare get afraid or at least upset.

"Offhand, I'd say he completely fell under your spell, while he secretly longed and craved for your romance in his fantasies, hoping that Mister Wyi Worri would think he was Godsend while he protected ordinance instituted by God, and promises taken in His presence to be forever abided; but you flagrantly betrayed on it with that fake reality… and that gave Prince Williams blind reason condemning him. He didn't care what substance this Mister Wyi Worri was made of, or what jealous issue this Mister Wyi Worri was talking about there."

"Let's take it this other way too; Prince Williams wasn't so nuts, after all. He must have watched that sentiment-like judgment, and started thinking rationally. I wonder if he remembered that first night your sexual groans were romantic torment to neighbours, and connected things to cloying dramatics. He sure did something… because in running over he found there was something there Mister Wyi Worri was helplessly lamenting upon. But like everything else, he made a mistake too. He wanted inviolateness of preordained union. He must have summoned you and admonished you the need why your waist should be kept pure and sacred for the indivisible union."

She was smiling again, and he knew why she was smiling when she should be pleading. She had been expecting this conclusion, and this conclusion left no room to cast her away in respect to what he had taken her to do in the inviolable presence of God.

"Your vow, it wasn't inviolable, though expected to be. Your matrimonial-kind of union can be inviolable or cannot. Lately… just few days ago… Prince Williams was able to tell a kind of if the vow that really instituted the union is disrespected and violated, the union itself is expected susceptible to be attacked… because it's now a dead letter, it won't be a sacrilege.

"And Mister Wyi Worri was able to tell God how he tried to caution you with the information He Himself had tried to give in each dream."

Now he had made her know he had even convinced God on his rescinding mission like open and shut case, her soul was going to crawl in the mud invariably. He felt all the strangling pain of disappointment at the heart. No! She wasn't worth his love. He had to make move now and find someone who would appreciate all the love he expensively gave. He went on talking; "You're a hypocrite of bottom of hell… maybe that's what best to tell you. Yeah, you're a damn crook of pit of hell. Everybody was ready to count Mister Wyi Worri wrong. You steered them seeing him as a basket-case. But, trust me, no matter how many spirits plotting a man's death, it'd come to nothing unless his personal god took a hand in the plotting.

"Hell, it was a pity for someone to see him in fools-paradise there, because he understood what the situation was like early enough… and he knew you were bolshy evil femme fatale."

Now she was blinking her eyes, perspiration was breaking out on her forehead. She moved away from the door and dropped into his chair, speaking to him in a low voice, looking down. "I know you understood what the situation was like, maybe early enough; but I know you didn't think it wasn't much better than it was. You didn't think me near evil of bottomless hell… because you actually told your inner self the truth I wasn't that it seemed."

Did she hit a point there in his head? A point on something subconsciously undertow about his being all along a self-appointed poodle? But his head was a mad frenzy of scrimmage shutting back and forth, too suspicious to settle with that smart point she was using like a soothing liquid washing away the iniquity of it all—to mitigate her treacherous heinous callous loose ventures.

"I know there were things you had salvaging thoughts, but your hot pursuing inkling was too fast to allow you settle with the inner truth," she said again. "If Double-chief wanted to be the one who marries me, and if a certain intolerable height of infidelity case happened to shake the relationship me and you had… firstly seeing a fed-up plaintive message from you, which was so like bust-up that it couldn't tell any information other than you were at the brink of freezing out… and secondly having you lose your common sense in a hot bid to revenge, he certainly would take advantage of that situation; don't you think? He could change status and twist stories following them, and you wouldn't be the wiser. A hungry lion will make friends with a hyena; he might have planned to kidnap and possibly kill you, but he saw your ingenuous credulity and thought otherwise.

"After all, it'd even be profitable to insinuate himself into that... keeping you out of the race, but under his crafty disinformation and chicanery. If my threat ever splashes on my rocky friendship with him, it becomes a situation both of you lose out entirely. It was such a profitable scheme that a monkey which goes out to grow horns returns with ears cut off. He mouthed out and lost out, and now I was able to keep my affection whole and focused. When you think of it, that one wasn't a good partner, but a worst rival a contender can have."

Now this was too much for him; he grated his teeth and dropped his head in his hands, pressing the hands against his face. *Aye, when a vulture goes to funeral, it sheds tears of joy*—that was what he forgot.

"That is..." she was adding; "if Murphy's law means anything to you. Did you ever wonder why I let your *'unsafe'* reference to my pussy get to me, cutting the naked wire responsible for limbic system of sexual response? I thought I could tell. Perhaps I'm still not too sure. But if you've accomplished all you planned for yourself on this, you've probably not planned enough... like you missed me all those while, I'll give you every chance to realize I missed you too." She pulled off her clothes and stood brazen naked. "Please, take off your clothes too."

He looked at her unbelievably; she meant it. She spread her hands in the air as an indication of total offering, and then put them down.

"Double-chief had a fiancée he had planned to marry soon when we met, but he was good and helpful and earned my good rapport, then he didn't want this lady again. But he was a friend and I was good to him and this lady, and they were my close confidants," she said.

He watched that story. Often he wondered why his cranky caller took the pains, and how she even laid hand on such high sensitive stories that should have been high rigid secrets. She knew what he was thinking.

"It tells about your cranky caller, and her wondrous sacrifice to help a stranger. I know it's described in that gossip packaged for your eventual visit," she said.

And she wouldn't be anything but right—

Yeah, the pieces came flying back together. They were all there and not making much sense, but there were enough of them so she would expect him to know she should know he would have it all someday.

Little bit of jagged information. Things like the way the cranky caller was getting uptight. It didn't tell of someone who wanted to help another, but someone who wanted another to help her.

Things like the way the cranky caller fell for his charm. It didn't tell of a lonely lady, but a jealousy lover who sought to redress the balance.

Things like then the way MyAngel went indefinably indefinitely mad about his *'danger'* reference to her lovemaking— of all his brazen accusations.

"Now I'll tell you why I let it of all the barefaced allegations, Mister Wyi Worri." Her voice came from a long way off. "I had to keep that costly claim to keep my conscience less scourging over the truth I'd nevertheless done evil to your pessimistic love… and this was exactly what I meant when I told you your insults have lost the impart they had once had. But I'd paid my most decent sacrifice… accepting pains of suffering silently, tolerating a case of infuriating harassments, to keep that you said was infected, for you and for you alone. I continued to put a smiling face to Double-chief because I knew he wasn't going to present our case the way it was, if he got to know you. I was never part of his twisted stories. You told me my pregnancy for you was a bent of nature, and I saw your unacceptability of your baby, the product of our love, in your feral unguarded character. I actually thought you didn't mean anything with your pre-nuptial vow, because having a baby and a wife was what you had all along dreamed. You'd wanted me to abort the baby and later had some scurrilous portentous dreams, that told you'd never loved to marry me… and you wouldn't say why you chose to distant me in your lovemaking. It was a long time, in fact, this time this case has all bust open this shameful way, before I found out they presented every frustration you'd ever saved up.

"I know Chinonso tried to come between us, and tried so much to resent her. When she started making mistrustful jokes about my body, I had reason to feel bad, but I let it go. I even let her get me some pills to all intense and purposes to take them along in my visit to you, in case we need them. But in your place I didn't make use of them again, on a second thought that this was a broody opportunity to have your baby. And that was the pills you saw in my purse.

"You see, I'd suspected something at the heat of your blind suspicion about the baby I was carrying for you, and I'd asked Double-chief privately to be a shoulder to lean, and told him enough about us, so that he'd have an idea what I was looking from him. He was hooked to Cyndi in the meantime like I said, but he started pestering me… and his love for her was dwindling. I knew you were doing the same toChrisette, but I still loved you and appreciated my choice of you. He didn't see your message himself, I showed it to him. Then when I didn't show up back to my place in Lagos early enough, he thought I'd finally left for you, and picked you up on phone, and had the knowledge I wasn't even yet gone for you. His deceitful and desperate wicked heart gave him a choice… kill him and shove him away from the way, or maybe get him hoodwinked into severing their love finally. He didn't know that you'd planned to let go any hope of me becoming your wife, anyway.

"I did it, Mister Wyi Worri. I'm not sorry for what I did. I induced the bloody relationship with him, and did the little hidden things behind you. But I didn't get any pregnant for him, and never was reckless with his relationship. It's just that darkness is so great it gives horns to a dog. I didn't yield to his proposal and never had an engagement with him. The day we came to my place we were from a burial ceremony at Umuahia, and I branched to see my mother. I heard he came back later, but that was his damned business. The night I told you I went to Ngookpala it was his place, and I went to pick a quarrel with his people against such move. During this time I found out your pessimism strengthened rather, and your love was a desperate shallow thing that needed just revenge." She swallowed some hard saliva. "You know little wonder we have a rare coincidence here. Cyndi told you a Richard, who's my ex… and this man I met that helped me on my journey home was Richard, but another Richard."

"Actually Prince Williams you said was your friend, had harmful love towards me. Yes… far from secret. It was shameless and brazen, without atom of regard for the trust you had for him. While you think he was a Godsend to protect our dear love, he was actually there harassing me for some messy love. But it would have to be over my dead body, and I knew his pestering me was a cheap cause I'd put a rout easily."

"You said he did all that?" Mr. Wyi Worri asked, but nodded knowingly. Yeah. He should trust her a little here. "Well, I shouldn't be surprised," he added nevertheless.

"I know." She watched him. "I let it be kept inwards in us like that, without mouthing it out, for two reasons. I know his love was too treacherous and despicable and creepy to even consider he could succeed about me. And, nonetheless, it was good you didn't hear me say it since your claim he was a protector of this love, somehow guaranteed your sustenance of this love."

He saw her go soft and move to him, take his hand, and then her hands closed on it.

"I miss your love… your touch, Mister Wyi Worri. Like you said, you know what the situation was like early enough. You know it was much better than it seemed… make love to me for the last time."

Now he saw those hands sliding around his waist—but he just stood.

"Love me the last time, because you wouldn't be my lover anymore. You know it; I can be your sister henceforth, but I'll not be able to be your wife anymore."

Aye, he knew it, and he had let her know it, but slowly he began to discard his night robe. "Yeah, I don't think I was such a patsy," he said; "I know quite well you weren't a bolshie evil femme fatale… I know you were better than you seemed."

Only the soil knows when the son of mouse is sick—she held him close. "It was just a case of living in cloud-cuckoo-land."

"Yeah… cloud-cuckoo-land, but with costly losses," he concluded.

They stood there unclothed, holding each other for the last time.

*F*orethought *And* *Preparation* *is* *necessary* *before* *embarking* *on* *affairs* *of* *life,* **Whyworry Books** *are* *superb and properly eliminate the cost of hindsight. They are books of fascinating insight that bring to the fore unbeatable foresight you actually need to forestall or foreshorten damage. Heaven forfend that my dear friends are encouraged to prefigure! Forewarned is forearmed. Grab these spellbinding novels that did something to help;*

1) **'In The World Of Eve'**
2) *'Weird World'*
3) **'Dark And Mysterious'**
4) *'Kill Frankenstein'*
5) **'Cloud-Cuckoo-Land'** &
6) *'Eternal Triangle'.*

Available on Kindle and other devices; Available from Amazon.com, CreateSpace.com, and other retail outlets.

—Emmanuel Nwachukwu
*Director, **Whyworry Books**.*

info@whyworrybooks.com
www.whyworrybooks.com
www.lulu.com/spotlight/whyworrybooks